RETURN TO THE TIME MACHINE

Author: © Adolfo Pérez Agustí

Contact: edicionesmasters@gmail.com

RETURN TO THE TIME MACHINE

The writer H. G. Wells builds his time machine and travels to the past with Humphrey Bogart and Groucho Marx, getting to know Mata-Hari, Picasso, Al Capone and discovering the treasures hidden in Tutankhamun's tomb.

This is the fiction story of a dreamer, the brilliant H. G. Wells, the first writer who dared to speak of a time machine, which could bring more benefits to humanity than any other invention.

CHAPTERS

WHAT HAPPENED AFTERWARDS?

Characters

H. G. Wells (1866-1946)

Herbert George Wells was born in 1866 in Bromley, Kent (England), and over the years became a popular author and political philosopher, especially for his science fiction novels that contain prophetic descriptions of the triumphs of technology, as well as the horrors of the wars in the late nineteenth and early twentieth century.

Author of more than 80 books, it is possible that his career as an author was caused by an unexpected event that happened to him as a child. In one occasion, he had an accident and broke his leg, dedicating all his obligatory convalescence to reading any book that fell in his hands. Then, Wells won a scholarship and completed his education at the Normal School of Science in London, where he developed a friendship with the famous biologist Thomas Huxley, who welcomed him under his wing, and who later on became a teacher. For this reason, it is likely that Wells' science fiction, a term he never used to define his style, was influenced by his studies at the Normal School and the special interest he developed in biology.

Wells soon achieved fame with his first fiction work, "The Time Machine", in 1895. Shortly after he published "The Island of Dr. Moreau" (1895), "The Invisible Man" (1897), and his greatest popular success "The War of the Worlds" (1898). Undoubtedly, the fate of Wells seemed to be already linked to the world of technology and science, trying to show a plausible vision of the future of humanity. He soon became an active member in the Fabian Society, a group of social philosophers in London who carried out more social criticism than science fiction literature, which led to the abandonment of the later. In his writing, he always tried to provide exact scientific data, although with a futuristic vision, perhaps too advanced to be admitted at the time.

It seems that his contemporaneous French colleague Julio Verne was one of his greatest detractors, accusing him of deceiving readers with his futuristic delusions, an opinion that was not shared by the critics of those days, who considered both authors very similar. Similarly, Wells accused Verne of writing only paper sacks, while he said of his British counterpart that the supposed scientific truths were only aberrations. Certainly the most fantastic scientific inventions were never made (especially The Time Machine), but the adventure and creativity with which he illustrated his stories provided great fun to several generations of science fiction fans.

HG Wells had two specific visions of the future of Humanity, one of salvation and another of judgment, and perhaps this grief made him obsessed with the possibility of creating a time machine, so we can consider that this novel is the one that best reflects his illusions and dreams.

Most of his stories were written in the late nineteenth century and opened a path not explored in science fiction literature. For many of his contemporaries, Wells was "The man who invented tomorrow", and now, at the dawn of the 21st century, we realize that his futuristic vision, between apocalyptic and real, is almost a fact. In his imagination, he saw cities crossed by wide freeways, excellent but overcrowded cities, computers, and machines to see novels instead of reading them, televisions to give live news, as well as the widespread use of tanks in war and the massive use of airplanes to bomb cities.

With his great ability to predict the future, in 1911 he talked about a new type of devastating weapon, the atomic bomb. In 1914, he published "The World set free" in which he anticipated to the political unbelievers the immediate destiny of Humanity, destroyed by uranium bombs, stating that if men did not change they would destroy themselves. However, and wishing to partially break with his catastrophic vision, he published some humorous novels, among them "Love and Mr. Lewisham" (1909), "Tono-Bungay" (1909) and "The Story of Mr. Polly" (1910).

Orson Welles (1915-1985)

Orson Welles was born on May 6, 1915 in Kenosha, Wisconsin, soon emerging as a prodigy child who rejected conventional education and who liked to perform tasks as a theater director. At the age of 16, he began his career as a professional actor in Ireland, later touring the United States with the company of actress Katharine Cornell, and later debuting in theatrical direction with an adaptation of Macbeth (1936), entirely represented by blacks.

Imaginative, ambitious and very daring, he managed to build a good reputation in the radio and the theater, in Ireland and later in Broadway, with his role as Tybalt in Romeo and Juliet. In 1937 he founded the Mercury Theater, where he produced innovative plays for radio and stage, including a radio recreation of the novel by HG Welles "The War of the Worlds", with which he managed to convince his listeners that the on All Saints Eve the Earth had been invaded by the Martians. The success, once past the hysteria, helped him to get a contract with the RKO, to direct and star in two films for 225,000 dollars, plus a total freedom to produce them and a percentage of the profits.

After several projects, he wrote with Herman J. Mankiewicz a revolutionary script entitled "Citizen Kane", initially called "American", based on the life of businessman William R. Hearst. The film, although considered a masterpiece over the years, was almost a commercial failure at the time of its release. Then he directed "The Lady from Shanghai" (1948), a film noir movie, in which he worked as an actor with his wife Rita Hayworth, although the filming was so rough that they divorced after a few months.

The following Welles film proved to be a strange version of Shakespeare's drama "Macbeth" (1948), in which the actors speak with a strange accent, leading to a new commercial failure. Adding to his misfortune, this same year he also has to leave to Europe to avoid being arrested accused of communism by the Committee of Un-American Activities, taking advantage to shoot films as disparate as "Othello" and "Mr. Arkadin ", the latter in Spain. "Othello" reached the Grand Prix of the Cannes Festival in 1952 and that award allowed him to return to the United States with honors shortly afterwards, once the witches hunt was over.

On his return, in 1958, he shot "Touch of Evil", a thriller with Charlton Heston, which is persecuted by moral censorship and represents a new commercial failure. Without losing heart and in his persistent attempt to show new forms of expression in film, he shoots "The Trial", an adaptation of Frank Kafka's novel of the same title with which he wants to demonstrate the false morality of society.

In Spain he plays "Chimes at midnight" (1966), based on a play by Shakespeare, as well as "Don Quixote" and "The other side of the wind", two works that he could not finish. Wishing to try his fortune in another country, he went to France and there he made for television "The Immortal Story" (1968), ending with "F for fake "(1973), a mixture of several stories narrated in the form of a documentary that also went unnoticed.

At the time of his death in 1985, he was completing his unfinished film "The other side of the wind", the project he had started in the sixties, leaving it unfinished again. With that story he wanted to tell the audience his own life, that of a famous film director (played by his friend John Huston), who tries to find funding for his film, something that Welles had to do numerous times throughout his lifetime. Sad end to a filmmaker misunderstood in his time and was raised to the category of movie genius when he died. While years later some of his films have been considered masterpieces and are among the ten best in film history, Welles had to dedicate his last years to working as an actor to survive.

Humphrey Bogart (1899 -1957)

Humphrey Deforest Bogart, who was born on January 23, 1899 into a prominent family in New York, began his career in theater when he was 20 years old, becoming over the years one of the most prestigious actors in Hollywood. At that time, most of the men of the forties began to imitate him, mainly through his character in "The Maltese Falcon" (1941), "Casablanca" (1942) and, somewhat less, when he won the Oscar for his great interpretation in "The Queen of Africa" (1951).

Although he was initially considered one of the typical gangsters of the 30s who appeared in the Warner Bros movies, it was later, before and after the Second World War, when "Bogie" became an idol. His anti-hero aspect, totally out of fashion, smoking and drinking non-stop, and seemingly cold with women, personified the image of the average American.

Although he sometimes played criminal characters, Bogart created an extremely rich and complex image on the screen that symbolized Hollywood's black cinema culture as a visual icon. With his embarrassed expression, the shadow of never having slept long enough, and the gentle swaying of his cigarette smoke, came to mean the cynical character who has to live in a gloomy world. For that reason his expression was of eternal weariness, a convinced individualist, slightly trusting with women and deeply honest; a very sentimental man.

When he was portrayed as a war hero, who discovers the horrors of the fight despite fighting in the ranks of the winner, he achieved a combination of traits that made him the romantic hero who fights for an ideal. And talking of romanticism, it is impossible not to remember his work in "Casablanca". Never a man could carry with such dignity that his beloved went with another in a flight towards freedom and happiness.

His image did not fade over the years and although aged prematurely by alcohol and tobacco, he was still equally powerful and capable of enthusing the new generations. Today, after almost 50 years of his death, he is still honored as the best representative of the complete detective who does not hesitate to express his opinion with phrases like: "Women are very simple: I never met one who didn't know what a slap in the mouth was or a 45 bullet means".

Julius Henry Marx "Groucho" (1890-1977)

Born on October 2, 1890, in New York, Groucho Marx is one of the few Hollywood actors who deserves to replace the Metro lion during presentation of the films. Imagine him with his mustache, his glasses and his cigar, greeting us before starting the film, while he sketches an ironic smile enclosed in a circle.

Each of his films characterized his unique talent, even in those sequences in which he only acted as narrator. His verbal interpretations with Chico, Harpo and Margaret Dumont (an impossible love, mostly because of the difference in size), are frequent reasons for stupor and comic delirium for the viewer, and one of the most interesting attractions in the films of the Marx Brothers. It is therefore not surprising that it has been frequently said that Groucho was the only one of the Marx brothers who managed to make the audience laugh, and some of that must have been true, since he was a comedian for 75 years while the others left the cinema quickly, once the group dissolved.

Groucho was never a relaxed performer. He cared very much about his show and always expected a disaster to occur, a feeling he also shared with Harpo. That's why, and if it had not been for people like Minnie (his mother) and Chico, Groucho's career would have ended at least a dozen times throughout his career.

When he was still a boy, he had a beautiful voice to sing and he worked sometimes as a soloist, although personally he did not trust his voice and for that reason, except for some melodious shouts and some song with his brothers, we have never been able to enjoy that pleasant voice they said he had, especially in his mother's opinion.

Someone claimed that Groucho really wanted to be a doctor -more specifically a gynecologist- especially one of those who had pretty nurses around him, although Minnie took that perverted idea from his head. As she was a frustrated artist, mostly because of how badly she sang and danced, she came up with the happy idea of introducing her children to the world of entertainment and, with a little luck, she would finally be able to see herself on stage and pick up some sneaky applause. From that day, the figure of Minnie accompanied the brothers wherever they went, although, in the end, all turned around the young Julius/Groucho, who always insisted in passing doctor consultation with girls, even if it was in a play.

Over time, this grump was the most famous of the Marx Brothers, mainly due to the popularity he quickly achieved with his work in the world of comedy. Groucho interpreted movies, narrated stories, wrote books, presented television programs, danced and even sang for many years, creating a school in which even today nobody has been able to take away the leadership. He won several awards for his work, including an Oscar, an Emmy, and the title of Master of Arts and Letters of France.

Groucho was also a consecrated author (having written six books already gave him that category -according to him- the first of them entitled "Camas") and a renowned screenwriter. In 1937 his work (written together with Krasna Normand) "The King and the Showgirl", had a great success. As they say, Groucho was happiest when he was working on one of these literary projects and that is why his books deserve a much deeper revision than his films. Of special interest are "The Groucho letters ", "Memoirs of a mangy lover" and "Groucho and me".

The end of Groucho's professional life was marked by the decreasing surplus value of the Marx Brothers, although over the

11

years there has been a revival of interest in his films. It is as if each new generation were interested in the work of these three brothers who made their ancestors laugh.

His personal life in recent years was overshadowed by the conflict between his son Arthur and his accountant Erin Fleming, who fought hard for control over Groucho's income, and finally for his will and the worldwide rights of his works. He was married to Ruth Johnson (1920-1942); Catherine Gorcey (1945-1951) and Eden Hartford (1954-1961), though from 1971 until his death in 1977, Groucho was sentimentally attached to his secretary Erin Fleming.

CHAPTER 1

1938: THE INVASION OF THE MARTIANS

In 1938, the company Mercury Theater created by Orson Welles and his friend Houseman, made a radio recreation of the novel by H. G. Wells "The War of the Worlds." On All Saints eve, the invasion of the Martians to planet Earth was broadcast, with Welles and his assistants telling in detail how they systematically destroyed all the cities. The terrible heat ray that was able to destroy cannons and tanks of the powerful North American army, plunged into terror and despair the, until then, quiet citizens, who panicked out into the street in demand of help, trying to avoid be victims of Martian power. But there were no Martians, no extraterrestrial ships, and no even destructive lightning; only the voice of Welles on the air warning every fifteen minutes that it was only a radio novel.

Once the frightened citizens were reassured, there was no shortage of protest voices demanding responsibility from those who had been able to terrorize an entire nation in the midst of hysteria of extraterrestrial invasions. With the planet Mars closer than ever to the Earth, and the UFO appearances mixed with the supposed attacks of the Russians, the population's fears did not need many stimuli to come out. For that reason and before the threat of serious denunciations by what was considered a gigantic fraud with spirit of notoriety, the director Orson Welles saw himself in the need to summon a press conference, to which also attended the creator of the novel "The War of the Worlds", Mr. H.G. Wells.

The place chosen was the National Arts Club, a private club located near Gramercy Park, specifically on the East 20 ND Street in New York. There were representatives of the magazines Variety, Photoplay and Metronome, as well as columnists E. Wilson and Louella Parsons, both famous for their lies about the behavior of spectacle people.

Although they shared almost the same last name, neither Herbert nor Orson knew each other and they were not even relatives, but soon there were many rumors that they were actually children of the same woman but different father, which was certainly not true. Any biographer knew that both had lived for most of their lives in different countries, but tabloids were aware that by making up stories they would sell more news than telling the truth.

-Well, gentlemen -Orson Welles began, addressing the journalists-before starting this press conference, I must clarify that I have been pressured by the county prosecutor to hold it. I have no interest in explaining to the public the reasons for broadcasting the novel "The war of the Worlds", and even less to apologize for having excited them. If there have been situations of collective panic, it is only because I know how to tell stories on the radio. In the same way that a father cannot be sanctioned for effectively telling the story of "Little Red Riding Hood", to the point of making his son tremble

14

with fear when the animal eats the unhappy grandmother, I do not find it reasonable to rise voices asking for my head.

-But Mr. Welles -said E. Wilson- you have not limited yourself to telling the story effectively. What he has actually done is to make the listeners believe that he was narrating news, exactly as it is done in the news.

-The history is like that. It is narrated in a documentary way by the author of the novel as if it was an event happening in our days, using situations and real characters. But that has been done previously by Arthur Conan Doyle or Edgar Alan Poe and so far no one has criticized them for it.

-I really think -Wilson insisted- you knew that confusing the listener would make a greater impact and deliberately used that trick. This is as if the President of the United States announces the attack of the Russians tomorrow and then says it was a joke.

-I feel flattered for being compared with the President, but I think I do not have as much influence as he does.

- Do not you think that from now on your popularity has reached similar heights? After all, you have shown us that you can lie as cleverly as any politician (laughs).

- (Sensibly angry) I see, Mr. Wilson, that you are as imbecile in person as you are writing, so now give me the satisfaction of not hearing your voice again and letting your colleagues talk.

At that moment and perhaps because of the great amount of murmuring, some insulting Orson Welles, H. G. Wells stood up and with his hands raised asked for silence from the journalists.

-Please, gentlemen, let's not turn this conference into a personal confrontation. The original story is mine and, therefore, if there is someone responsible for this collective hysteria, it is me. It is me to whom you should address the criticisms.

-But Mr. Herbert -spoke conciliator Louella Parsons- nobody has criticized the validity of his novel, so extraordinary that I think we have all read it. Personally I heard the recreation that Welles did on the radio and I must admit that he fascinated me, although of course I never thought it was a real event. The problem was only announced as a novel at the beginning of the broadcast, but from that moment everything was narrated as if it was a real event. That is why those listeners who tuned in to their station after the introduction fell into the trap and believed that it was actual news.

-Well, that is not condemnable and I hope that if you radiate my novel "The Food of the Gods" or "The Island of Dr. Moreau", do not fall into the same trap. Radio is a means of expression in which the imagination of the listener is vital to attract their interest, but to stimulate that imagination you have to use some tricks like those used by my friend Orson. When the protagonists kiss on the radio everyone knows that it is pure fiction, the same as when we heard the flight of Superman or the adventures of Flash Gordon. I think you should applaud Mr. Welles, instead of criticizing him for having managed to confuse the listener.

-As far as I understand - the Variety correspondent said, rising from his seat- you claim that anything is valid to shock the listener on the radio in order. That seems shameful to me, since they justify anything if they gain audience with it.

-It is you -said Orson Welles furiously- the least suited person to criticize me! as you work for a magazine that enjoys inventing stories about actors and actresses, not hesitating to defame them if it helps to sell more copies. At least I have not defamed anyone and my characters are fictitious ... unless you consider the Martians real (laughs in the auditorium.)

-My magazine -he replied, even more irritated- usually publishes rectification notes when we have given some false news, but...

- (Welles, interrupting) Well, they're going to need an extra number every week to apologize. You are the one who should be at my post responding to the attacks. I am a radio professional who knows how to do his job perfectly, just as H. G. Wells did when he wrote his novel. People like you, always eager to publish false news, are the ones that really cause harm.

At that moment, all the journalists were already out of their seats, gesticulating loudly, and the calls to concord that H. G. Welles made were not effective. Only the presence of the two policemen who watched the events prevented the punches replacing the insults, especially because Orson Welles insisted on boxing with the representative of Variety magazine. Still significantly altered, both colleagues went out through the back door, where a car that would take them to their homes awaited them.

-Those cretins -Orson Welles continued- believe they have the right to defame those they wish. At least I have been able to enjoy telling them what I think of them.

-Yes -Herbert replied- but tomorrow his name will be on the front pages of all the newspapers and not just to mention his work on the radio.

-It is important that they talk, even if it's wrong. It would have been much worse if my program had gone unnoticed. Now at least, and for free, everyone will know that there is a filmmaker called Orson Welles.

-I have the impression -he answered with an undoubtedly prophetic sarcasm- my friend, that it will not be the only time your name will appear on the front pages of the newspapers.

-That comment, coming from a writer who talks so much about the future, I find it instructive. I hope your forecasts are fulfilled. Certainly, I am convinced that both his scientific forecasts, like those of Jules Verne, will end up being a reality.

-Included the invasion of the Martians or The Time Machine? He asked wryly.

-I do not know if they will be the Martians or someone from a nearby galaxy, but just as the peoples of Earth have been invaded on numerous occasions, it is very possible that some alien feels the same impulses. It's all a matter of someone knowing that we exist and having something that might interest them. What I cannot believe is the travel in time. How can you travel to a future located thousands of years away by simply putting a date on a clock?

-Well, I have included the watch in my novel so that the trip was accurate and easier. My main idea was to talk about the fourth dimension, that place that never changes even if the dates and circumstances change.

- But you are convinced of the possibility of traveling in time?

- Going to the future I do not see many possibilities, but to the past yes.

- And where is the difference?

-The future is something that does not exist and possibly never exists. No one knows if tomorrow will be alive and if that great city will remain there or will have been destroyed by an earthquake. However, the past is something real, something physical that existed and that still remains present. All the sounds of years ago, the lights, the heat and the cold, or the movements of people, have been transformations of matter, have not disappeared. They are scattered somewhere in the universe waiting for someone to restore them to our time.

- (Putting some interest in the conversation) I understand. It would be like listening in a tape recorder to a voice recorded years ago. The person who spoke at the time may already be dead, but his voice remains there, as expressed.

-Exactly -he answered passionately upon hearing Welles's reply. The cinema and the sound recordings are a perfect example to explain my theory about the time machine. These two systems in a certain way take us to the past again and again, to the real past, since that which has been printed or recorded was authentic, it is not fiction. The films have been impressed by luminous phenomena emitted by the characters or the elements, while the voice is also a transformation of the matter and can be stored in a suitable device. In a thousand years, humanity will be able to see and really hear what happened in the past and they will be making a comfortable journey through time.

-But, even so, there are still other elements missing for this experience to be real. We have sight and hearing, but there is no possibility of touching, smelling and tasting anything of the past. Personally -he imagined with a smile- I wish I could have an affair with Queen Cleopatra, preferably inside that bathroom with donkey's milk.

- That jump in the so far time is now impossible - it said something disillusioned, while it outlined without enthusiasm a smile - but now it exists the possibility of traveling to nearer times.

-It means that it finds it feasible that in the future someone could invent that time machine...

- (He straightens up and says proudly) my friend Welles, I think the time has come for me to be honest with someone and I think you are the most appropriate person.

-You talk to me in a way that scares me. What are you hiding from me?

-Nothing that your fertile imagination has not already sensed. The time machine that I described in my novel is not fiction, and even less an utopia; right now it's totally finished in the basement of my house.

-Dear Herbert, I see you intend to sell me something, but I must warn you that after the disaster of tonight I do not think I can get a penny. You are a nice person whom I admire, but I have not yet entered into that delirium of taking you for a God.

- (Beginning to shrink again, while retaining his pride) Mr. Welles, I am already an old man of 72 years old, tired of living in a fantasy world and eager to be taken into account for more than being a visionary who writes novels about the future. I have been waiting for a long time to find someone who deserves to share with me the great experience of traveling through time and that chosen person is you. Do you think that I have come to your press conference only to defend you before the journalists?

-Well, in a certain way you are also guilty of the crisis of hysteria of that radio novel. -If your story had not been so descriptive and disturbing, no one would have believed that my novel was a real fact. Anyway, I would like you to continue talking about that time machine that claims to be a reality.

- (Taking him by the arm) If you have time, come with me and I'll show you. My apartment is not far from here.

CHAPTER 2

THE TIME MACHINE

Both went down the street; now well into the night, while on the way H. G. Wells explained the technical details that led to the construction of that alleged time machine. His enthusiasm was already contagious and he did not even wait for confirmation to be believed.

-If you have read my novel "The Time Machine" -he began to explain- you should know that although I talk about the fourth dimension as a place of space-time which can be reached easily, I do not explain how it can be achieved, nor I mention technical details about the time machine. I simply describe the invention as a vehicle equipped with a chair, a very simple control panel, a wheel that is the engine that moves us in time and a strange crystal that is supposed to provide the necessary energy. But I do not explain any scientific data, since it is pure fiction to travel to the future.

-Then, what is the difference with the machine that you now pretend to have built?

- (partially trampling his words) It is about traveling to the past, to a place that already existed and whose physical presence circulates somewhere in the universe. The future is not written, that is true (hesitates for a moment), or possibly it is, but the past is perfectly described and of the events that took place a few years ago we have photographs and recordings. Simply looking at a photograph, we are already making a visual journey into the past.

-But the physical element would be missing, the one that would allow us to get back to that time.

- (With new energies) Think for a moment of what a photograph is: an instant of the past that has been stopped forever. From the moment that the photography was impressed, the future began, but we have already managed to stop that moment for a second, which we now consider the past. (Keep talking without waiting for an answer, although now trying to simplify) When I started thinking about what would be the way to be part of that real visual element I came up with a crazy idea, well, at the time I considered it so, but that took me to a step already into the trip in time. By the way, have you read that story entitled "Mary Poppins" by Pamela L. Travins?

-As much as "Peter Pan."

- Do you remember how they make the first trip to a world of carousels and merry-go-rounds?

-I think it was just entering a painting painted on the floor that contained that imaginary world.

-Well, now imagine that you could enter inside a photograph. That he found the means of integrating himself within that image and merging with it using x-rays.

- (Smiling) But we need Mary Poppins to make that miracle come true..

-Well, Miss Poppins is now my time machine.

Orson Welles still had his mouth open, not so much in amazement as in the urge to laugh, when they arrived at Herbert's house. Crossing a small garden, in which there was a sundial, they entered a Victorian house, walled in walnut wood in the most traditional English style.

Without making any further comment, Herbert led Welles into a well-lit cellar, almost entirely occupied by a strange cylindrical dwelling.

-Here is my time machine," Herbert proudly showed.

-Well, I admit that your strange device is impressive when you see it -he said, opening his eyes significantly- but I'm sorry I do not share with you that conviction about the possibility of traveling to the past through a photograph. I'm too heavy -she pointed to his body smiling- and big enough for something like that. Anyway and giving it a bit of credibility, I would like to know if you have already made a trip to the past with this artifact.

-Two, and they were a total success! He said shouting. If not, I would not be asking you to do my third experiment with me now.

-My God, dear Herbert! Is it possible that you have thought that I have believed you to the point of getting into that machine with you?

-If you do not believe me, what is your fear? What can happen to you for doing the test?

-I do not know, it's possible that we died electrocuted. In addition, these X-rays do not offer much confidence and I have read that their radiation can be harmful to health. Are you sure you have already made two trips to the past?

-I have no doubt about it and a proof of the safety of my machine is that I am now here, speaking to you, completely healthy and conscious. The first time I tried to find out only the possibility of traveling to the past and for that, I used a simple picture I had made a day earlier in Central Park. I put it in the machine, I activated the whole process, and in a few seconds, I found myself in the same day and place of the photograph, with the same climate and with the people that were in that moment around me.

- You never thought that it was simply an illusion?

-I must admit that I always considered that possibility and had to rule out that everything was an optical illusion or a process of hypnotism induced by the machine. When I entered the time machine I had the photograph taken the previous day that faithfully reflected that moment, in addition to my watch that marked the time and day of the moment when I activated the time machine. There was, therefore, a date that was not going to be altered.

-Well, what happened? He asked, intrigued. Did it not provoke any hysteria among the people of the park when it suddenly appeared before them?

-Nothing. Everything is done so quickly that even the human eye cannot catch anything strange. I found myself in the same place where I had taken the photograph and nobody was able to perceive my sudden presence. It was a strange feeling and for a moment I thought that everything was a dream, but in reality I was still living the existence of the previous day and that my time machine was the product of my imaginative delirium. I must admit that I was the first to doubt it.

-What made you to believe it?

- (Blunt) My watch. It marked the same time and day when I entered the time machine, that is, a day later. A look at the newspapers that were for sale told me without a doubt that I was in the past.

-I'm a little dazed with your explanation, because I got confused when is the past and the future. What did you do then? How did you return to the present?

-I simply let the effect of the machine pass. I had made my measurements so that the trip hardly lasted ten minutes and after this time I returned to the interior of the machine. For me, that experience had taken only a few minutes-my watch attested to that-but when I returned everything was as before, without even a single second having passed. It was as if the current world had stopped at the time of my trip. A day later -he continued speaking, certainly excited- I went back to the same experiment, now using a photograph of the Statue of Liberty that I bought in a gift shop. I appeared abruptly among the tourists, with a jump back in six months, and this time I stayed half an hour.

-And again, back home...

- Yes, but now I needed new proofs about the veracity of my trip. During my stay in the Statue of Liberty I bought a newspaper published that day and I took a flower from the place to carry both objects until my time. The possibility of bringing treasures from the past was too tempting not to try.

- (Anxious) Well, and where are they?

"I do not know -he answered with noticeable disappointment- perhaps lost somewhere in the fourth dimension. They did not return with me, which now seems logical to me. Those objects could not travel to the future, in the same way that I cannot do it either. As belonging to the past and since it seems clear that the future is not written, they could not appear at an improper time.

-Well, my dreams of bringing Cleopatra back with me have vanished- he said with some sarcasm and no less disappointment.

-And also to be with her, since it is impossible to travel until that time so far.

-I do not get it. If the machine allows you to travel to the past, what is the problem to travel to ancient Egypt?

-Transmutation can only be done through a photograph and that scientific advance belongs to our century. Unfortunately, we need a real material to travel to the past, a painting cannot be used as it does not reflect reality. The painters used the eyes to capture the luminous signs, but their hands, paintings and brushes were instruments that altered the objects represented.

-It seems logical, but what I do not understand is how to integrate into a photograph.

Come on, I'll show you.

Not without some uneasiness and suspicion, Welles entered with Herbert into that great oval cylinder, completely lined with mirrors and which seemed designed to house several people. Inside, the atmosphere was pure and a strong smell of electricity indicated the presence of some high-energy generating machine.

-Look, just behind where we will stand to make the jump in time there is an X-ray machine, an instrument discovered in the last century but that was not perfected until a few years ago, precisely by some friends of mine called Lane and Braggs. This wonderful device emits invisible electromagnetic radiation, with a higher frequency than ultraviolet rays and has two fundamental properties: it can pass through bodies, and later print a photographic film.

- I have heard about it and about the many applications it will have in medicine to explore the interior of our bodies. I must admit that his invention is starting to interest me.

-I'm glad because I want you to carry out my third trip to the past with you.

-My Friend Herbert-Welles cut him off nervously- you know that I'm an admirer of your novels, but do not take me for a guinea pig.

-Well, do not refuse it until you know the characteristics of my invention. What I can assure you is that there is no danger for us and that the device always automatically returns to our time.

-You keep talking and then we will see if I really will accompany you.

With more detail than Orson Welles needed and could understand, the inventor of the amazing machine ran through every corner of the machine, sometimes too artisanal to make it look like a scientific project worthy of the name. Even so, he explained with pride the interest he had put in achieving a sealed compartment, inside which the intense radiation generated was not lost to the outside, at the same time that a scrupulous polishing of the walls allowed to bounce the rays and concentrate them only on the time travelers. There was also a huge and precise clock, with the date and the present year, to give testimony of the exact moment in which the trips to the past are made, thus leaving a record of the trip. All these details were explained with a growing enthusiasm by Wells.

-Once the X-rays are in operation, they will go through a photograph, the one we have chosen, and they will project that image into this cathode ray tube, similar to the one they are using in televisions. However, the key is in this wheel, a particle accelerator, through which we accelerate the electrons with an electric field and with another magnetic we direct them towards the cathode ray tube.

-I hope that this new invention to watch movies at home does not destroy the entire film industry.

-Don't interrupt me, please, because now comes the best. In the middle, we will be placed between the cathode ray tube and the photograph, and we will be crossed by X-rays. From that moment our matter joins the photograph and both are projected in the cathode ray tube, so fused in a single image that it is impossible to differentiate ourselves. Then we will travel to the same place and time that was in the picture at the speed of light, so our own body particles do not have time to disintegrate and recover in another time and place.

-As simple as that?

- (somewhat annoying) Simple? I have worked seven years to build this machine and it seems simple to you?. Electricity or the flight of an airplane also seems simple to us now, but three hundred years ago they were only chimeras of the dreamers. No, my friend, there is nothing simple about my time machine.

-Well, do not be offended, although I still do not understand your invention in its totality. Another question that comes to my mind is about the return to our time. If the time machine does not travel with us and remains in this basement, how can we get back?

-Actually, I do not do anything in this sense. The image that is recorded in the cathode ray tube travels through spacetime, similar to how the television images travel, but they are not perennial and their effect is temporary. I would need a source of energy greater than the electricity so that we could remain weeks or months in the past. According to my experiments, the electrons that move inside that tube are unstable and need a very intense light source to be united. Maybe in a few years someone will invent more powerful electric generators, although surely I will not be alive to improve my invention.

There was a dramatic silence at that moment, without either of the two men being able to break it. The tremendous initial illusion of one, Herbert, and the cautious curiosity of the other, had immediately disappeared at the possibility that this invention was lost forever by something as natural as death. But that comment must have been the motivation that Orson Welles needed to decide to undertake the journey through time, since he told him vividly that he would accompany him now.

-Give me only half an hour to go to my house and warn my parents -he said, heading for the door. I need to take care of some issues, but you already have a travel companion on your time machine for the next trip. By the way, where will we go?

-We'll travel here, to the New York of 1934. I have a photograph of the premiere of a play entitled "The petrified forest", and I'm curious to see the beginnings of that actor called Bogart. He has a great personality and charisma, and I feel that he will soon be very popular.

-I must confess that I have never seen Bogart work like that, but as a theater amateur, I would love to see that popular work live. By the way, -he added as he left- do you know what they say about Tymbal in "Romeo and Juliet?."

-I'm sorry I was not in that moment to applaud you, but possibly we made a trip there to check your virtuosity as an actor.

-Well, that will be incredible. Me, as a spectator, seeing myself in the limelight. In a way, I am afraid of that possibility. Have you not heard of the paradoxes of time?

-We will have time to digress about scientific issues and about the possibility of influencing the destiny of Humanity. Now the most important thing is that you come back as soon as possible to make the trip.

CHAPTER 3

AN ACTOR CALLED
HUMPHREY BOGART

Orson Welles was enthusiastic, although still suspicious, about making that leap into the near past. Eager to clarify his doubts as soon as possible, he went to his home to put his work in order and, of course, to bring a suitable clothing to such an experience. What he had not yet defined was the explanation he would give to his parents for such a sudden trip, aware that talking about a time machine and attending a theater performance four years earlier was not something that could be assimilated in a few minutes. Fortunately, when he arrived at his house his parents were not there and breathing relieved he checked the mail to organize his work when he returned. There he found a letter with letterhead of the RKO, which he opened hurriedly, since it was not usual for a film producer to take him into account.

He nervously tore the envelope and read the text:

"Dear Mr. Welles, we have received good reports about your work on the radio and your ability to make innovations in the world of entertainment, qualities that fit within the renewal policy of our company. As you know, we have premiered 'King Kong' with extraordinary success and we have two new projects for which we would like to have you as director and protagonist. The first one is about the life of tycoon William R. Hearst, whom we know you hate in the depths of your soul. It would be called 'American', although there are those who think it would be better to change it to 'Citizen Kane'. The other script is entitled "The Magnificent Ambersons" and would feature the performance of Joseph Cotten. For both jobs you will receive $ 225,000 and the possibility of joining our regular directors. If this offer is of your interest, please contact us at our offices within 24 hours to formalize the contract. Sincerely, David O'Selznick, Vice President. "

He could not believe it. In less than two days he had shocked the world with his radio serial "The War of the Worlds", was about to make a trip to the past in a time machine, and had just received the best job proposal of his life. Apparently, there were too many emotions together for anyone, but for Welles they only meant incentives and confirmations of their creative capacity.

The lateness of the night -it was almost eleven o'clock- prevented him from going back to Herbert's house to ask for a 24-hour postponement in his journey to the past, since this was the time he needed to go to the RKO's studios to sign the contract. Somewhat disturbed by the events, he left everything properly ordered in his house and went to bed with the intention of visiting Herbert early, from where he would go to the film studios.

Meanwhile, Herbert was already impatient - almost grumpy - for the return of Orson Welles, although it was clear to his mind that he would not make concessions to anyone, knowing that it was difficult for anyone to really believe in his time machine. The minutes became hours in his imagination and enraged by what he considered a lack of ethics and respect, he went to the basement with the clear intention of starting up his time machine. He would do the trip alone as he had done previously.

He placed in the appropriate place the photograph of the stalls of the Lyceum Theater, made during the premiere of "The petrified forest" in 1934, and started the generator that was to activate the X-ray device, in addition to light the tube rays cathode and the photoelectric cell amplifier. In the middle, and without any additional protection, H. G. Wells, again in his journey to the past, although now it should last at least, according to his calculations, three hours.

A blinding light flooded the cabin, amplified intensely thanks to the reflective coating of the walls, and in a few seconds a new image appeared projected on the cathode ray tube. The light signal was already traveling to the past and with it H. G. Wells. On the way, and by a fate of destiny, Orson Welles had missed the trip.

The human figure of Herbert materialized just at the end of the hall of the Lyceum Theater, now in darkness as the play was on, so no one noticed his presence. Aware of the need to go unnoticed, he sat in one of the few available rear seats and attended excited the performance of "The petrified forest". There they were playing Leslie Howard and Humphrey Bogart, the latter performing the wicked Duke Mantee, the gangster who had no mercy with his enemies and who had now become a kidnapper of innocent people.

The applause of the public interrupted the performance several times, while Herbert, still stunned to be able to witness such an event, could not beat his hands to participate with the enthusiasm of the public. When the show ended, he had only one obsessive idea in his mind: he should take this moment to meet Bogart in person. Discreetly, as innocently waiting for someone to realize he was a time traveler, he went to the dressing rooms and asked the janitor to greet Bogart and Howard. Although this pretension, to see the actors personally, usually leads always to failure, a business card with his name was enough to open the way to the dressing rooms. Fortunately, H. G. Wells had been a famous writer all over the world for a long time.

Mr. Wells, what a joy to greet you! Leslie Howard said, stepping out of his dressing room and reaching out to shake it. Your visit is the best thing that could have happened to me today.

-The pleasure is mine. I have been willing to meet you for a long time now.

- (Bogart smiles) I hope you have not come with any Morlok. Where is Weena?

"I think I've missed something -Howard said, wondering- Who are you talking about?"

"I see -said Bogart- you have not read "The Time Machine" by H. G. Wells. On his journey to the future, he meets a beautiful young girl whom he falls in love with, but then he has to rescue her from the wicked Morloks, some inhabitants of the underworld who love eating the unhappy inhabitants of the surface. It is an exciting work.

-I must admit I'm not a science fiction enthusiast- Howard admitted ruefully- but I became an admirer of you ever since I read "Dr. Moreau's Island". The possibility of doctors manipulating animals and people to get applause and money seems abhorrent to me. His story left me deeply worried and since then I have gone much less to the doctor. Well, why don't we continue our conversation in the cafeteria around the corner?

And here there were three men gathered that time would turn into legends of art, each one so different that it was impossible for them to have anything in common. Fortunately, the philosophy of Wells and the verbiage of Bogart, were reason enough to make the conversation something unprecedented and exciting.

-I cannot understand why people get angry- Bogart said. You cannot live alone and to discuss you need two people, but if they do not agree with each other always the discussion starts. Yes, and nobody starts a dispute saying: "Oh, of course, you're right!", Or, "I recognize that you know more than me!"

-I have the impression that you- Howard accused him- like the controversy a lot. Personally, I do not enjoy arguing with anyone and prefer to find a pleasant conversation with someone who agrees with me.

-My idea of a discussion -Bogart continued- is to start by explaining each other opinions. Then, when the other says something like, "you're a real fool," is when things start moving in a practical sense and I'm sure we'll get to an understanding soon.

-I see you like both the confrontation and your theater characters-
Wells replied with a smile. I'm not sure if you have been infected by
the characters or you have found your twin brother in Duke Mantee.

-Oh, do not believe for a moment that my desire for controversy
always ends up being so peaceful. On one occasion, in this same bar,
I was with my later wife, Mary Phillips, and a guy approached us
and said: "I heard that you are a tough guy, but that must refer to
another person because you don't seem as tough as they say" "You
are right -I replied. Why don't you sit down, my friend, and have a
drink with me? -The man accepted the offer but continued: "Do you
know that I have been told about you? He does not want to sign
autographs to children"

"It was obvious, -Wells interrupted- that this man only wanted to
fight, not talk.

There was no doubt about it. But I did not want problems with
anyone, so I took Mary and we left. The guy got up and said: "Just
what I thought! That he would run away. You make me laugh, you
are not a tough guy. He grabbed me by the shoulder and we both
ended up rolling on the floor.

- And who won the fight?

"My wife," he said, with a discreet smile. Yes that is correct; She
took off a shoe and inserted the heel on his head several times. I
think that guy still walks down the street carrying a unicorn horn as
a reminder of that day.

-I see that your character in the theater corresponds well with your
personality- Wells commented mockingly.

-I think that this dry character, if I have it, I owe it to my mother. The last kiss I received from her was when I was only seven years old. I caught a pneumonia that left me on the verge of death and that disappointed her so much, because she considered me a child so strong that diseases could not overcome me, and from then on she stop caring about me.

-You should not talk about your mother like that -Howard mildly criticized- I'm sure she loved you even more when you were sick.

-I cannot say that I love my mother; maybe I admire and respect her, but of course it's not the kind of affection that would serve as a model for a love movie. I do not even send her gifts on Mother's Day, because I'm sure she'll send them back. When we see each other, instead of kissing me, she slaps me on the back and encourages me to continue working as an actor.

- Do you have that same relationship with your father?

My father just died a fortnight ago.

-I'm so sorry! -Wells apologized-. I think I should not force you to talk about family issues.

-Don't apologize. Actually, we people need to get our internal demons out so that they do not corrode us inside. I have great memories of my father and he is the person I have loved the most in my life. We used to go fishing and, even though we never caught a single fish, we would go to the same place because he wanted to be away from my mother. His death came suddenly, while playing chess with a friend at a local on Sixth Avenue. They took him home at his own desire and died in my arms. That is when I realized everything I wanted, although I have the satisfaction of having told him that I loved him before he died. I know he heard me because he looked at me and smiled. He was a great man and I am sorry he had not lived longer so that he could have seen me work in this magnificent work.

-Well, my friend," said Leslie Howard, "if it is true that there is another life, your father will be proud of you, since I have good news to give you. I have received a letter from Warner Brothers in which they ask me to perform in the movie "The petrified forest", along with Bette Davis and Edward G. Robinson. I have answered that if you do not play Duke, I will reject the work, and they have accepted.

-I see that there are still good friends.

-Well, you do not applaud me too much. Actually, I have plenty of offers and that's why I have allowed myself the luxury of pressing them to work with me. I have also received proposals to play the main role in "Pygmalion" and they have given me a novel entitled "Gone with the Wind" to read. There is a very ambitious project to take it to the cinema.

While this conversation was ongoing, Wells nervously looked at his watch, aware that the time of permanence at that time was coming to an end. As if he was a male Cinderella, he knew that he only had a few minutes left to go back to the future and he had to do it in a solitary place, without the presence of witnesses. Soon he found the most credible and easy excuse.

-If you forgive me for a moment, I would like to go to the toilet.

And so, when he had hardly entered one of the booths, the time machine returned him back to the year 1938, as safe and sound as he was before the trip to the past. Gone was the experience of having been able to meet two such extraordinary actors as Bogart and Howard, although now he was already hoping in his mind to return to visit them without the need for new trips in time.

He was again at home, inside the time machine, still hot from having been running almost three hours in a row. Reviewing his experience, he knew that he still had many doubts to solve, and the most disturbing of all was the possibility that all these experiences were nothing more than a hypnotic trance induced by X-rays. The question was also posed that the theory of the parallel universes was a reality and that although it had been in the past, these facts will not be reflected in its own time and existence.

He had to leave doubts and for that, he urgently needed a companion, someone to confirm everything that was happening. After washing and changing clothes, he ate the dinner prepared by his faithful housekeeper, and hurried to the home of Orson Welles, anxious to tell him his new experience. There he received the discouraging news that he had suddenly left for Europe and that they did not expect his return until a week later; too much time for a person as old and restless as H. G. Wells. Aware that death was already around him and he could not afford to waste a single day of his life, he hurried home to plan his next trip in time.

CHAPTER 4

THE CORRECT AND THE INCORRECT

Now he had a priority goal: to see Bogart and Howard again so that they would confirm the meeting that had happened four years ago at the Lyceum Theater. Other types of projects also went through his mind, including traveling sixty years into the past, when he was a child, to regain the emotions of his childhood, with his parents still alive and the world immersed in the plans to enter the twentieth century. Since he had some photographs from that time, the trip should not be a problem, although he was seriously worried about the possibility of being face to face with himself, little Herbert. He did not know what could happen if he modified his own destiny, or if he could actually do it.

He was also attracted by the possibility of changing the most important historical events of Humanity, such as the murder of Tsar Nicholas II and his family, or Archduke Franz Ferdinand during his official visit to Sarajevo. He wanted to prevent, if that was possible, the fortuitous sinking of the Titanic, to meet Lenin and Karl Marx, shake hands with Charles Chaplin, orient Lindbergh on technical details for his trip across the Atlantic, and why not?, take all the money deposited in the North American stock exchanges a day before the collapse of Wall Street. He also wanted to prevent the unstoppable power of Hitler, who had just annexed Austria to Germany and rumors came to him that he was trying to seize Czechoslovakia, Poland and the Soviet Union. He was worried that since they made Hitler Chancellor in 1933, this 44-year-old Nazi had managed to get all communists out of the weak German democracy and take over absolute power. The United States wanted to remain on the sidelines of what they only considered as political "little conflicts" in Europe, but he, like good English, wanted his country to maintain its independence forever.

It was not easy for Wells to make a correct decision about what his mission was in this life, now that he seemed to have the possibility of influencing the destinies of Humanity. He was aware of how limited he was, because although he knew the events that would happen until 1938, as well as the details and the people involved in them, he did not have the right to correct weapons, money or powerful friends. A 72-year-old man traveling to the past would not be more credible than any fair fortune teller, and would most likely put him in a tenebrous asylum before he could do something positive to change the events. Sad crossroads for a person so eager to bring such an important legacy to Humanity, even more discouraging because all the decisions had to be taken alone. He urgently needed one or two people (more could not travel in the time machine) to, at least, share doubts and purposes. His feverish imagination took him to anguished extremes, warning of the imminent danger to some people, while this same warning could suppose the death of others. If he sent anonymous to Tsar Nicholas II concerning the people who were conspiring against him, this would mean the immediate execution of Lenin and Trotsky, and without them the subsequent Russian revolution could not take place. The destiny of that great country would be therefore unpredictable, being at the mercy of Germany that would, thus, achieve the greatest empire in the world. Nor would it be of much use to approach the English shipping company White Star to warn them that this vessel they considered unsinkable would sink precisely on its inaugural trip, along with more than half of its passengers. No one would believe his predictions and could even be accused of sabotaging and causing the sinking of that ship when the event took place. How could I explain that I knew the sad outcome of that ship thanks to a time machine invented several decades in the future? Surely, millions of people would request their immediate processing, and possibly their summary hanging.

He had to calm down and plan better his next trips, avoiding too much interference in the destinies of Man, even if they were sad. The first thing was to look for company and I was sure that Humphrey Bogart would be the perfect companion. Therefore, he chose the ideal time and place for a new meeting: the wedding of Bogart with Mayo Methot, an actress who was said to have a devastating right to resolve conflicts. The news had been published in Variety magazine and they even described the place where it would be celebrated. And so, that August of 1938, Wells and Bogart would have a new encounter in which it would be clear if the previous trip in the time machine had been a reality or a fantastic dream.

The response was immediate, because once the machine was activated and Wells transported to the interior of the house of Bogart, as it appeared reflected in the photograph, and although Wells remained seated among the guests at the wedding, trying to be taken by one of them, Leslie Howard saw him at once and hurried to greet him.

-Mr. Wells, how great to see you again! When Bogie finds out that you are here at our wedding, he will be delighted. We tried to find you and meet again after that meeting we had at the theater, but it was impossible to contact you. No one could tell us your address and we thought you had gone back to England.

-True, I had to leave quickly and believe me that I was sorry not to say goodbye to you. A problem arose suddenly and I did not have time to leave my new address.

- Ah, time! There is no way we can control it as we would like.

-Don't believe it, friend Howard, it's not that difficult to have the time in our hands. It's a matter of knowing how to backtrack on time.

-But the clock never stops; it is so inexorable, reminding us that we are mortal. If we could go back and live again in the past, who knows where you and I would be now?

-Possibly right here -he replied with marked irony - trying to plan our future.

At that moment Bogart arrived with his new wife Mayo, as beautiful as apparently irascible. His expression was more like that of a young man trying to get away from his girlfriend to go out with friends than a newlywed, supposedly dazzled by love.

-Dear Herbert, you do not know how pleased I am to see you! I am glad that you are at my wedding and so you can accompany us to the party we have organized. May I introduce you my wife Mayo, the most charming of mortals and the only one who can make me stop smoking from time to time.

-With both, alcohol and tobacco -she said- it is possible that I will be left without a husband very soon. I believe that I will establish a League against Drinking Husbands. Do you know, Mr. Wells, that my husband and Errol Flynn are not accepted in many luxury restaurants?

-Maybe it's because they do not like food and protest very strongly- Wells replied, trying to be nice.

-Not at all. It is because when they take more than two drinks, and in his case we could say ten, they run all kinds of damage in those places.

-OK! Interrupted Bogart with a certain brusqueness. But I think sometimes it's better to drink a lot before going home with certain wives. It is difficult to get home knowing what awaits us and, in addition, to make it sober.

-Friend - said Howard, becoming cordial in the midst of the new married couple, I think the time has come for you to kiss as newlyweds and keep your differences for when you are under the covers looking for each other.

This small war between the two newlyweds dissolved with the same rapidity that had been generated, and they all went to the newly opened house of the Bogart, where the bustling wedding banquet took place. Among the attendants to the party, there were Spencer Tracy, Errol Flynn, Samuel Goldwyn, Alan Ladd and Bette Davis, as well as numerous friends not so popularly known. But for H. G.

Wells this whole world of personalities did not excite him and he only wanted to be alone with Bogart to talk to him about his time machine. He had so many projects and so many possibilities to live lost events, that he could not delay his new trip any longer. Bogart seemed to disappear abruptly, but soon found him sitting in the small bar of his private restaurant, reading a newspaper.

- Do I interrupt you? Wells asked.

-Not at all. I was reviewing the film billboard, because I have not been to the movies for a long time and I want to know what's happening around me. There is a film that I would like to see in particular, since I keep a good memory of its protagonists. I see that the "The Cocoanuts" of the Marx Brothers are still on display, and I think this may be a good option.

-I must admit that I have not seen any movie of them, maybe because my sense of humor is not so deranged. I've always been an admirer of Chaplin and Buster Keaton.

-Well, I think the time has come for you to enjoy this trio of comedians and this is a good opportunity. As I find weddings, including mine, very boring, we will sneak out through the door to the garden and surely nobody will miss us.

- Not even your wife?

-My wife? Look at her well: I think she has just started her dance number 59. When we were first introduced to each other, she claimed she danced more than Ginger Rogers.

- And you do not like to dance?

-Not even on top of my enemy. Well, come on, I think this is the time to start a subtle retreat in search of Groucho Marx.

And just as they had planned, it happened. The two friends sneaked out the back door, heading to the cinema where they projected "The Cocoanuts". There they occupied a discreet chair and Bogart's laughter ended up passing on Wells who, disconcerted with himself, covered his mouth not to show that also the delirious comedy of the Marx had taken over his senses. When the movie finished it was almost dark and they slowly started the way back to Bogart's home.

-Bogart, are you not worried that the violence of your characters is a bad example for the audience? It's as if you gave them ideas to commit a crime.

-I do not think that cinema can induce crime. When I was young, news about Billy the Kid were often in the newspapers, but that did not increase the number of criminals among my friends. If someone wants to find out what makes children delinquents, they should look at their environment, and particularly their family life. Parents who allow their young children to stay in the street until night, are the only ones responsible for making them delinquents later.

- Do you think that the actors can have some positive influence on the education of people?

- Sooner or later I will be a father and for that reason I am very interested in youth violence. The problem is that the public is fascinated by gangsters and the reason is their great popularity. The police try to stop them, with many cars, the National Police and the entire FBI, to hunt them like rabbits and shoot them so much that even their mother would not recognize them. But then that police is not appreciated because it is associated with an army that prefers shooting, instead of stopping the ringleaders. When a mafia boss escapes he becomes an idol, a person who has managed to circumvent the police siege. Then he becomes a nice murderer.

-I think it's true -Wells added thoughtfully- for history is full of examples in which the offender is more appreciated than those who live an honest life. See the example of Robin Hood and Pancho Villa, two people worshiped in their respective countries for stealing and killing the enemy.

-But this is not a good example, since these people did it as an act of justice. They had to hurt the powerful people to benefit the poor people. It is not the same as Al Capone or Bonnie and Clyde, people who have only pursued their own benefit without caring who they were hurting.

-Exactly -Wells insisted - but surely more films will be made about these criminals than about Edgar Hoover, the director of the FBI in charge of catching crime professionals. If you were to play a loving husband role you surely would not be reaching such popularity.

-Well -he replied with some sarcasm- they have also congratulated me on the way I kiss the actresses. The truth is that we cannot always choose the roles we would like to interpret. Possibly we cannot do anything to influence our destiny.

- Do you really believe that destiny is written? What would you do if you could go back to the past and have the possibility to rectify?

- Herbert, talks of a subject that I have raised on numerous occasions. If I could go back to live, I'm not sure that I would do things very differently from how I did them. We behave according to the circumstances and that's why when we look back we usually justify ourselves in almost everything. What I am sure of is the things that I would repeat, like being close to my father. My life has never been scandalous, I have never come to the brothels, nor have I persecuted virgin girls. I have not smoked drugs nor have I sought to appear in the press. If I went back to living my young years I would continue to behave like that, because it is part of me.

-Are you willing to make a bet with me that if you lived again you would not behave the same?

-Of course I'm willing to bet, but I do not understand how I'll be able to prove anything.

-You just have to come with me to my house -he said enthusiastically, grabbing his arm. There I will show you that people are never satisfied with what they did in the past, except on exceptional occasions.

-I'd be happy to accompany you Mr. Wells, but I think if I do, my wife will practice boxing with my nose when I get back.

-Do not worry about it -he said, grabbing his arm even more firmly. We have all the time in the world to return without her missing you.

-You really like to talk about time; No wonder I wrote that novel about traveling to the future.

-And the past, my dear friend Bogart, and the past.

52

CHAPTER 5

IN SEARCH OF YOUR DESTINY

When both friends entered the basement of H. G. Wells, where the monumental time machine was anchored, Bogart's pragmatism was like a jug of cold water for the great inventor. No sign of amazement, no rictus of surprise and not even a desire to find out the usefulness of this strange device. For all answer he asked if he could give him some whiskey, because he found his throat parched.

-I've talked more in the last few minutes," he said, "than in my whole life. If I do not refresh my throat as soon as possible i will need the fire service to come.

-I'm sorry to disappoint you, but I'm not a drinker and the only thing I can offer is sarsaparille.

-Sarsaparille? How awful! That is for Mexicans.

-Well, they say it stimulates the manly faculties of man.

-Now I am already excited about that sarsaparille. Better give me the bottle without delay, since I expect a night of intense love with my wife. That is if she does not receive me with a slap for arriving so late.

-Do not worry; you will arrive in time to enjoy the pleasures that your wife will offer. Tell me one thing: if you could return to the past, even for a few minutes, where would you go?

-Well, that depends on if I had a single occasion or I could repeat the experiment. If I could choose, possibly i would like to meet some beautiful woman from the past, such as Cleopatra or Lucrezia Borgia.

-But these women -Wells argued- have not only gone down in history because of their beauty, but sometimes because of their wicked behaviour.

-Well, an attractive and passionate woman in love cannot be asked to be also benevolent and tolerant. Personally, i'm content if she is able to take me to the seventh heaven every time I kiss her.

-But are there no other women who you like equally, but who have gone down in history for their literary or humanistic legacies?

-Well, I also find interesting the princess of Eboli, you know, famous for her many lovers, or the dancer Isadora Duncan, who was said to have as much skill dancing as taking off the seven veils.

- I believe that the Duncan was not famous for removing veils and you confuse her with Mata-Hari.

-Mat-Hari? The Nazi spy who danced naked? That's an interesting woman! Imagine her stirring the pants of her lovers in search of secret documents while kissing them passionately.

-I see that the sarsaparille is taking effect. By the way, I think I have a photograph of Mata-Hari during one of her performances at the Folies Bergère in Paris, although she still had not removed the seven veils.

Stirring in his properly messy photographic archive, where he accumulated hundreds of photographs from years ago that would serve as a guideline for his trips to the past, Wells had serious difficulties finding a photograph of the famous French spy.

-Do not tell me -Bogart said impatiently- you do not know where that picture is kept with the naked dancer. These documents must be carried in the wallet and used in moments of sadness and loneliness.

-I think our assessment of women is very different- he said, still searching for the photo.

-For me, women are very simple: I have not met anyone who did not know what a slap in the mouth or a 45th bullet means.

-If I did not know you, I'd think you were a convinced misogynist.

-I've lived two divorces and that's why I do not have much confidence in the kindness of women. Each of my ex-wives has embittered my life in their own way and with great enthusiasm. They were only interested in my bank account and in controlling my free time. When they did not get any of the two things, they asked for a divorce ... and my money to live with their lovers.

-But you will also have your oddities, right?

-I am aware that I am not socially accepted in general. I do not show enthusiasm for the tastes of people and I detest parties; that's why I think people are afraid to invite me to their homes. They may think I'm going to talk nonsense or fight with someone, when in fact what I like the most is that they leave me in a corner with a glass of whiskey in my hand.

- (Wells keeps looking, almost without paying attention) Being nice will not hurt either.

-People think that by being an actor I must have a great charisma at parties and be the perfect host, always willing to play and laugh bad jokes. I'm not a clown in charge of brightening people's parties. If they want to boast of having talked to a popular character they should look for another more affordable one.

-Look, here's the picture! I'm sure you'll like it.

Certainly the image had to please him, since Mata-Hari was there, totally naked, in the middle of a decoration that simulated a Hindu garden, mounted on a white horse richly adorned with authentic turquoise inlays. It seemed like the prize to any man who had the privilege of winning it. Bogart looked at her with enthusiasm, though showing that he was used to holding equally beautiful women in his arms.

-Do not believe that my thoughts are always linked with the women of the past. There are moments in history that I would have liked to live, and one of them is the European war against Germany -said Bogart, trying to be something more transcendental.

- But you did not fight during the First World War?

-The war began in 1914 and I joined the ranks in my country in the spring of 1918. At that time the American forces were fighting under General Pershing and my destiny was a ship called Leviathan, in charge of the troop transfer. The armistice was signed three months later, so I did not even get to shoot my rifle.

- And that scar?

- (Stroking his upper lip) I would have liked it to be from a piece of shrapnel from the enemy, but it was not from that. I was made by a prisoner whom I escorted to Portsmouth Prison. He asked me for a match and while I was looking for it he hit me on my mouth. At that moment he managed to escape, but I chased him and I managed to stop him. When I finally went to a doctor, the wound was already beginning to heal and my lip was slightly deformed -he said as he looked at the clock. By the way, I think it's about time I leave.

-I would like to show you my invention first. Come with me.

- I insist on the bad temper of my wife. When she realizes that I have disappeared from the party, she will immediately prepare an uncomfortable sofa for me to sleep on.

Both friends entered the time machine and that was when Bogart began to be aware that this was much more important than he thought.

-What is this weird thing?

-This thing -he said, suppressing his indignation at the comment- as you call it, is a time machine.

- The same one that you describe in your novel?

-It has the same purpose, travel in time, but technologically is not the same. It has no clocks, no comfortable armchairs and there are not even colored lights; those accessories are only part of my imagination. To travel in time you need a suitable technology, the same one that I used to build my machine.

-Are you trying to convince me -inquired Bogart, now annoyed- that this machine can lead us to know our future? You should know that although I have drunk enough, it has not been enough for me not to realize a joke.

-I'm not kidding friend, but certainly this machine cannot take us to the future. At the moment it will allow us to make a trip to the past, for example, to see in person Mata-Hari that attracts you so much.

- (Logically, without believing) I do not understand the purpose of this conversation, but I think the time has come to leave to take refuge in the arms of my newly released wife. If you excuse me ... (leaving)

-Please wait! I would like to show you that I am not trying to deceive you. Come with me and we will make a trip to Paris in 1917, just when the Americans had just declared war on the Germans, already intervening warily in the First World War. Maybe you have the chance to contribute a bit in that confrontation.

-If that was true about that time machine, the offer seems tempting. (analyzing) Pursuing Nazis and having an affair with Mata-Hari is more attractive than going to the parties that my wife organizes.

-In am sorry but you will have to solve the issue of the party yourself because the time machine will return us just at this moment.

-But if we travel to the past -he mused aloud, a little less skeptically- and we are there for a few days, that time will also pass now. The problem is that if I return to my house after a few days of vacation, right now that I just got married, I'm not quite sure of my wife's response. Probably she will have already mobilized the mafia to find me.

-Time travel will take several days -Wells assured him enthusiastically- but that trip to the past will not influence our future since it is something that does not exist yet. We are always leaving behind the past and working for the future, if it arrives.

-I do not understand this reasoning, and personally I have always believed that the only interesting and real thing is the present.

-I'll give you a simile: imagine you're watching a train full of wagons pass by. The machine has already crossed and we will call it "the past"; the central wagons will be "the present", and the wagons that have not yet arrived are "the future". What I want you to understand is that the future is nothing, except for a purpose, a foreseeable event. That hypothetical machine may never happen. For this reason we can only remember or return to see the past, in the first case with the mind and in the second with some element, such as a photograph or a movie. All our acts have already left an indelible mark on time and as all matter there is the possibility of recovering it.

-Well, it seems clear as you explain it to me, but I do not understand that today is not modified if we go on holiday trip to old Paris. If we travel to the past three days, that same time will pass now, in the present, and when we return we will be three days older.

- (Patiently insisting) Reconsider the idea of what is present and future, and you will realize that we cannot alter what does not yet exist. For that reason you and I will return at the same moment we start the trip and for the rest of the people we will not have disappeared for a single second. Do you want to take the test?

-Despite this scientific gibberish I am not a man who is afraid of risks and adventures, so go ahead.

A little leery, but quite convinced of Wells' good intentions, Bogart entered with him into the time machine, adjusted now for a trip that would last several days. The inventor placed the photograph of the Folies Bergère on one end of the apparatus, graded the X-ray beam, increased the power of the current generator-allowing it to run smoothly for longer-and lit the cathode ray tube. In the middle of everything were our restless friends. Wells, on the other hand, and thanks to his previous experiences, he already had enough money on him, a pistol, ammunition and a watch to specify his new trip. The machine started up, the powerful beam of light came through the photograph and our friends came out, melting everything inside the cathode ray tube in a crazy dance of electrons.

CHAPTER 6

MATA-HARI

As expected, and mixed among the public, there were already in the Folies Bergére Bogart and Wells, both somewhat stunned by the trip. Certainly the most disconcerted was Bogart, who looked around for a signal to indicate that everything was a montage, as is done in movies.

-If this is the filming of a movie, he said, I must congratulate the decorator; it is perfect.

-This is reality, my friend. Soon I will show you.

The Folies Bergère was not a very large party hall and therefore provided a great sense of comfort among the attendees. With dozens of cigarettes smoking at the same time and a motley mix of chairs and tables full of drinks, the atmosphere was very intense, to which we had to add the discreet red lights that barely managed to break the gloom of the environment. And there, at the back, on the stage, was a pretty naked woman sitting on the back of a white horse. Possibly more dazzling than ever, Mata-Hari was even more beautiful in the spotlight than in the photograph. Soon she got off the horse and started her sensual dance which she called "Devandasisher" and which, according to the publicity, she had learned in her younger days when she was confined in a sacred Indian temple. I wore a pair of earrings that belonged to a priestess of Shiva and who were the cause, she said, of her good fortune in life.

There was not a single male spectator at that moment who did not have his eyes on her, in her undulating body, while the few female attendants tried to find out her secret to achieve that unstoppable seduction with men. The conclusion that could be drawn was that not only was the nude, something that any of them could do without problems, but his naive look and not too bulky body, binomial that gave her a charm impossible to resist to. In the minds of men it meant something to model, to adore, just as the sculptor Pygmalion did before and that Bernard Shaw immortalized in his famous novel. But in her way of looking and moving there was something more than a simple woman who knew the weaknesses of men. There was sagacity, intelligence and pride to know that she was admired. His way of looking at her future preys indicated that to reach it would cost a lot of work ... and money. In exchange for it, pleasure without limits.

- What do you think of that woman? Wells asked.

-Sensuality is not learned, it is born with it, and that woman has it. She puts the cake before us, but she also tells us that only a privileged person can eat it. It is an egg that will only be penetrated by one among millions of sperm. Undoubtedly, she is a very smart woman.

What would you do to conquer her?

-What I would never do is to offer money. Love is not bought.

-But sex is.

-You can have both without having to pay for them.

-Yeah, for you it's easy because you are an actor and you are used to dealing with women. But look around and you will see that most of these men are unhappy people who have not received a kiss in the last hundred years. They only have the resource of paying if they want to get to hug a woman like her.

-Don't get confused Wells, we're talking about Mata-Hari, the goddess of love, the Dawn Girl. She is more a product for the fantasy of men than a solution for true love. There are thousands of women who can make us vibrate with excitement and passion only by showing us a naked shoulder, and that, in addition, they are wonderful companions in everyday life.

-(Hesitating) I hope your wife is like that with you.

-Now that I just got married and I'm so far away from her, I think I still have to work hard to find the perfect woman.

Suddenly, both stopped talking to look carefully at the proscenium of the Folies Bergère. At that moment something was happening. Four French policemen shouted and gesticulated with one of the managers of the premises, who struggled to prevent them from going on stage. Meanwhile, Mata-Hari had left hurriedly without anyone noticing it. In a few seconds, the small resistance of the local employee was overwhelmed and the four policemen took the stage, while asking with their hands silence to the public.

-Silence please! said one of them, shouting. We have to communicate something very important to you. Miss Mata-Hari is accused of espionage against the French government and of helping the empire Austro-Hungarian. Recently she managed to escape from the allied forces that had deported her to Holland and we are obliged to stop her to judge her in our country.

While this conversation took place before the incredulous eyes of Bogart, Wells was pushing him aside, taking him discreetly to the exit door.

-I think it's important -Wells said, almost whispering- that we leave as soon as possible. We arrived just at the time of her arrest and if they do a raid, they will surely also take us for spies. We do not have a passport or safe conduct, and we do not even have any reservation in any hotel.

-But we're Americans -said Bogart- and we can prove it with some personal identification, like a driver's license.

-That identification belongs to two people of the future and according to the document, now you should be 18 years old. Imagine yourself in a French police station trying to explain to gendarmes that we have traveled in a time machine.

- I still cannot believe that we are in the past. All this is the product of the imagination of someone who wants to play a joke on me.

-You are not famous enough for someone to go into so many troubles for you. Either you accept it or not we are now in the Paris of 1917, twenty-one years in the past. And now, let's go because surely there are more reinforcements coming.

The Folies Bergere soon became a tumultuous place, with people shouting, some to demand to allow them leave and others because of the stomping of the crowd. What until a few minutes ago was a place of pleasure and reverie, had become a disaster in which the weakest were having the worst part. The police, now with new and more energetic reinforcements, beat without mercy all who tried to confront them, while other agents already blocked the exit door. The shootings started and the first bodies flooded the ground. Meanwhile, Wells and Bogart had already gotten out and were running down the street in an unknown direction.

-Where can we go? Wells asked, almost out of breath.

-You keep running without stopping until we're well away," Bogart told him, shoving him roughly. Then we will see where we can hide.

-Hide? For what and from whom? If nobody knows that we are here they will not find us.

-Two people running always instill suspicion.

-And why are we running?

-Because it is an elementary survival rule. First we run and then we stop. As simple as that.

The right moment to stop was marked by Wells, because of his age he was exhausted. He had to hold on to a lamp not to fall face down on the hard and paved ground.

-Where we are? I do not know Paris at all, -Wells said nervously, sweaty and with a thin voice.

-We've run so far that I don't even know if we've done it right or left -Bogart said, reading a sign. Here it says "Rue Fontaine", but with my limited knowledge of French, it is as it said "Quinta Avenida".

-Don't forget that I'm English and that French is almost my second language, -Wells said, trying to reassure him. That sign means something like "Fountain Street", but the name is not so important, right now we should find a place to sleep.

-Hey, wouldn't be better to go back to our time? I think that by this time we have had enough emotions. I'd rather be in my wife's arms now, even if she doesn't have the same curves as that Mata-Hari. I think it's time to start up your time machine, but in the opposite direction.

-Unfortunately I do not have that magic key that you ask me. My time machine will take us back to our world in three days, October 17, just when the battery power runs out.

- Are you crazy? Three days in this hell? Bogart yelled, undoubtedly upset.

- But didn't you say that you wanted to live the emotions of the war and to help fight against the Germans? Well now you have the opportunity to do so.

-I was talking about fighting with a very powerful American army at my side,-he said resignedly -with their guns and tanks; not to be lost in a strange country, persecuted by all the French gendarmerie for having seen a naked dancer.

CHAPTER 7

MONTMARTRE

Both, already more calm, continued walking through the dark Parisian streets in search of a hotel. The area was now steeper, although in the background many lights were visible and with them the possibility of finding people awake and a free bed. A shouting, this time of people singing and laughing, led them to a bar called "Maison Catherine". The pleasant summer night of Paris invited them to sit on the small terrace of the place, in search of relief for their parched throats.

Sitting down - more concretely, lying down - in the wicker chairs, our friends decided to remain silent until they recovered their breath and calmed down a bit. A waiter approached them and asked them what they wanted to drink. Although Bogart made an intention to ask, a look from Wells was enough to silence him. Wells, speaking correct French, ordered two beers and cheese after explaining to the waiter that they only had dollars, because they were Americans.

-Well, dear Herbert, tell me now what we can do here in Paris, for three days and within the Fascist invasion,-Bogart asked, somewhat annoyed.

-If you knew more about history, you would know that Americans are welcome in France. We have supplied the French with food throughout the war, we have broken our relations with Germany and Bulgaria, and we are collaborating militarily with London and Paris. At the moment we are not spies, but very well considered allies because we have declared war on Germany on April 6.

-Well, but we are still tired, hungry and very dirty.

-Okay, I'll ask the waiter if he knows of a nearby hotel where we can spend the night.

When Wells returned, everything seemed to begin to normalize in this adventure. In this same place there were free rooms and they could spend the three days left until their return to 1938. When they went up to their room, they barely spoke and laid down in bed, they slept peacefully all night. The next morning, the cool breeze that blew on the Montmartre hill woke them up almost simultaneously. Arranged, cleaned and physically replaced, the two passengers of the time went for a walk around, but not before being warned by the owner of the pension to be careful with pickpockets.

-Two American tourists -he told them- are always a desirable prey for thieves. Keep your dollars in your socks and do not trust anyone.

The abrupt hill of Montmartre was the place chosen by the European painters to make their best pictures, although most of those who lived there, or lived poorly, were simple enthusiasts and dreamers who could never sell even one of their paintings. Crowded into small but charming garrets, with no more light than the one that entered the corroded windows, they spent most of the day painting the same landscapes again and again, in search of that style and peculiarity that made them suddenly jump to fame. Those streets had already been walked, in search of an unprecedented place to capture in their canvases, by painters like Van Gogh, with his red hair and his incipient madness, perhaps provoked by hunger. Toulouse-Lautrec was also there before taking refuge forever in the Moulin Rouge, where he managed to be accepted by the prostitutes and recover his confidence as a human being despite his short stature.

All these painters, in addition to Cèzanne, had contributed to providing Montmartre with an aura of legend throughout the world, and there was no student of the fine arts who did not consider it necessary to spend some years of his life there, between hunger and romanticism. Moreover, for those who returned to their countries the stay in Paris was already the highest prestige, increased by the possibility of maintaining intense love in which pain and sadness were the most common.

- Do you realize, Dear Bogart, that we are living an unrepeatable time?

- (Sarcastic) I agree with "the unrepeatable", because I hope that the next time we travel in time we do it to more quiet times and places. If you decide to travel to Hawaii, do not forget to take me a ticket in preference class.

- (Without listening to him) I'm worried about Mata-Hari. According to the story, she was shot here in Paris on October 15, in two days, and I would like to try something to avoid it. Since we know the fatal fate that hangs over her, it seems reasonable that we try to save her.

-But if history tells that she died that day, It should impossible for us to alter it.

-That reasoning I have raised several times, but I think there is a possibility to change the course of history without altering events. What we know is that Mata-Hari was shot that day, but that's what historians have told.

-I do not understand the difference.

-It is very simple. Suppose that everything was a simulacrum and who died that day was another woman who resembled her, or that in fact the bullets were fake, totally harmless. The historians were deceived like the rest of the population, because they described faithfully the execution and the death, although Mata-Hari did not really die. We could make that true, helping her escape death.

-Well, it's a possibility, but so far-fetched that it should not be considered. Right now we do not know where Mata-Hari is, nor who his friends are, or how we will manage to arrange the farce execution.

-You are a film actor and you are used to the sets and to pretend. This is your chance to do something real, even if no one is going to applaud you.

At that moment, the headlines of a local newspaper, shouted by their young salesman, got them out of doubt as to the fate of the pretty dancer. The news on the first page said that Mata-Hari had been detained by the French Intelligence Services and that the summary trial would take place that same afternoon. The phobia generated at that time against the German spies had been primed in her and was employed as a scapegoat by the government to give a warning to the real spies.

This stunned our friends who, seeing their attempts to save her frustrated, returned to their little attic. There they lay down in bed demoralized, meditating on the few possibilities offered by time travel, even if the cruel fate of things and people was known. Suddenly, voices, coming from the room next to theirs, took them out of their thoughts. Two men were arguing heatedly, conversation that could be perfectly heard through the thin, cracked walls.

-I have not taught you how to paint -one shouted- for you to do this crap!

- Crap? I am trying to provide my paintings with a novelty, a more daring perspective of what I see.

-What you do has no quality. Any child could paint it, or even a monkey if we gave him a brush. Nature is as we see it, not square and with unreal colors.

-This is what everybody else does and it is boring such a realistic style. If we do not bring new ideas to the painting, it is better that we dedicate ourselves to unloading bundles in the springs. I have not come from Spain to do what you all do, so discreet and purist that you bore the most enthusiastic art lovers.

The conversation grew louder, some struggles were heard, and Bogart thought it was time to intervene, mostly to protect himself against the possibility of the police coming. Jumping from one balcony to another entered the place of confrontation and there they found the two men, one younger than the other, holding both a painting. While one tried to throw it out the window, the other struggled to save it from disaster. The arrival of our friends put an end to the fight and now, both calmer, tried to explain the problem.

Look friends -said the eldest of them- this young man you see here is prostituting the art of painting with his paintings. I would not mind much for him, but as a teacher my prestige would collapse if his horrifying current paintings, unknown style, came out of this room.

-That unknown style -the young man replied -has a name and is called Cubism, and it represents the form of pictorial expression that will revolutionize painting. You, dear Monet, belong to the past and I am the future.

-Insolent Picasso! -shouted-. How dare you criticize who has taught you so much?

When the guy called Monet rushed back to the other man again, Bogart stepped between them, asking them again for serenity. Since the English language was completely unknown to the two painters, it was sufficiently revulsive to stop them again and to decide abruptly to end the fight.

-Allow me to thank you for your timely intervention -said the older of the painters. My name is Claude Monet and, although something old for these fights, I still think that painting should reflect reality, even improve it if possible. My friend and disciple Pablo Picasso was until now a good painter with a great future, but suddenly he has changed his style and has started to do what he calls cubism and that is incomprehensible in my eyes.

-I just want to try new forms of expression -Picasso answered, much more calmly. I am 36 years old and I need to create my own style, although in principle it is incomprehensible to others. I want to follow the line marked by other painters, and personally I am guided by Paul Cézanne, who affirms that all forms of nature start from the sphere, the cone and the cylinder. I am convinced that this art presents an analytical and abstract approach to the subject, allowing to provide new feelings and emotions through the use of geometric shapes and colors, without the need to reflect anything concrete. It is the lover of painting who must put his imagination. In this way, the viewer does not simply watch my picture passively and can let his imagination fly.

-The idea seems suggestive to me -Wells said, almost in perfect French- because that's how we turned the fan into part of our works. (He pauses) Let me introduce myself: my name is H. G. Wells, I am an English writer, and I must add that, just as Mr. Picasso has done with his painting, I have also made a great turn to my novels. I totally abandoned the realistic and social stories to get into the world of fiction and fantasy; That is why I understand Mr. Picasso's position. I think that all artistic styles can have their place in society, both the realist, the impressionist or cubism.

- And your partner is also a writer? Monet asked.

-No, he is a film actor who is starting to gain popularity in North America. His name is Humphrey Bogart, but he does not know a word of French.

-Ah, the cinema! Said Picasso excitedly. It is the most complete form of artistic expression of all. In the movies, all the arts are gathered at the same time. I am happy to be able to shake hands with two people as interesting as you. And what is the reason for your visit to Paris?

Wells was glad that Bogart did not understand the question, and much more accustomed to telling fantastic stories, he answered hastily but without hesitation:

-We are looking for scenarios to shoot a movie based on a novel of mine titled "The Island of Doctor Moreau". Unfortunately, the European war will prevent us from continuing with the project and we will go back to the United States in a few days.

-Certainly -said Picasso- this war is getting longer than expected because of the Kaiser. His cruel fascism is causing the ruin of all Europe and many innocent people are being shot every day right here, near the Palace of Justice.

- (Wells, realizing he can be sincere) Yesterday we witnessed the capture of the dancer Mata-Hari in the Folies Bergère. Had we not scape the place they would have captured us too.

-How? Interrupted Picasso, extremely upset. Mata-Hari has been imprisoned by the gendarmes? We have to do something to save her; she is a patriot, not a spy. Do you want to help us?

- Both my friend Bogart and I will be happy to do what we can to help her. However, keep in mind that we do not have a passport and that if the police arrest us they can also accuse us of German spies.

-Don't worry, I must also remain hidden from them because I am a member of the Communist Party. Wait a moment and I will try to find out where they have taken Mata-Hari.

Picasso left hurriedly, while Monet complained to Wells that at 77 he was no longer in good condition to run around the streets escaping from the police. However, he offered to collaborate with them to the extent that his forces allowed it. There was also a confrontation between Wells and Bogart, since the news that Picasso was a communist displeased him greatly.

-I do not like Communists -said Bogart angrily, addressing Wells. They try to undermine everything good that we have achieved in my country.

-But you have stated on many occasions your defense of freedom of expression.

-And I'm still in favor, as long as it does not mean destroying our own freedom. The press must be free and each citizen can manifest his preferred political idea, but this does not imply that they can meet clandestinely to form an army. I do not know a single communist country that has a good standard of living and liberties. That should be enough to exclude them from my country.

-Well, there are many people in the world of cinema who have openly manifested themselves as pro-Communists.

-And I still say that they are free to do it and think as they wish, but they should exercise their policy in Russia.

They were interrupted by the return of Picasso - now extremely nervous - who told them that they had taken Mata-Hari to the Palace of Justice and that they would probably condemn her quickly to serve as a warning to the spies.

-Surely -he continued, saddened- they'll execute her tomorrow. They have the habit of making quick judgments and shooting the guilty in a square on the banks of the Seine.

-And what can we do? Wells asked with little hope, knowing the fate of Mata-Hari.

-For instance we can go to the trial and then try to rescue her before the execution. Let's go!

CHAPTER 8

THE CADALSO

Bogart and Picasso, the youngest of the group, walked quickly towards the Palace of Justice and a few meters behind they were followed by Wells and Monet. When they arrived, the trial had not yet begun, but the courtroom was already full of people, some anxious to curse Mata-Hari and others to try to applaud her. Our friends looked for the best positions they could, finding a barrier of stout policemen that prevented any attempt to free the beautiful dancer. The feelings of the spectators were already very different from what they had felt in the Folies Bergère. A few days before, that woman was admired and applauded, desired, and she set the example for thousands of women who sought to escape anonymity and misery. Now, treated like a vulgar delinquent, it was going to be shown as scum before public opinion. When Mata-Hari came to the dais, handcuffed and dressed to the feet, escorted by the police, her haughty image had not disappeared and for many she was prettier even than in the spotlights. At the trial there were no witnesses to testify in her favor and there was not even a defense lawyer to apologize. Everything was already prepared in advance. They accused her of having loving relationships with the German officials and passing them on, in the intimacy of the bed, vital information about the movements of the French army.

-I've been frequently with soldiers who paid me to sleep with them -Mata-Hari began- since I'm not interested in men who are not in the army. I have also loved many of them, but I have not asked them about their nationality. I am attracted to the military especially because they are brave, adventurous and in some way superior, but when they are naked in my bed, nobody talks about politics and they only show interest in my body.

These sincere words did not serve to excuse her and instead sharpened the spirits of the judges, now also became censors because of the pressure of their wives, jealous of the attractiveness of Mata-Hari. No one defended her there, not even the same men who had loved her a few days before. All converted already into their enemies, she was accused of passing secret information thanks to her earrings. Shown in the room, they discovered a secret compartment in the back, where it was supposed to keep their warlike confidences. Naturally, at that time there was nothing in them, but for the judges it was the irrefutable proof of her crime. Part of the public became aware of the farce of that trial, especially because most of the people who passed as witnesses to the accusation were the same men who had had intimate relations with her. It was obvious that they wanted to destroy the proof of infidelity towards their women and this was their best and only chance. Her friends, now turned into enemies, alleged that she had served as a spy for both nations, France and Germany, depending on the side of his lover.

-Yes, I'm certainly a whore, but I've never betrayed France- Mata-Hari replied, crying.

The judge who presided over the court rose without flinching and said: -Margaretha Geertruida Zelle, alias Mata-Hari: has been accused by this special court for her crimes against France by acting as a spy for our German enemies and therefore condemned to die publicly shot. The execution will be held tomorrow in the square of this same Palace of Justice. May God have mercy on her soul. Not a single cry of repulsion for the sentence was heard in the room and instead hundreds of voices spat all kinds of insults at her. Only four people remained silent before this manifestation of injustice, endorsed by a court that was precisely there not to condemn any innocent. When everyone left, most to celebrate with champagne the next death of Mata-Hari -probably in the Folies Bergère-, Bogart had already prepared a plan to rescue her, inspired by some of his films.

-My idea is this: we need two suits of the French police and some false documents. With them, and if luck does not turn the back on us, we will be able to rescue Mata-Hari before her executioners realize it.

-And who will put on those police suits? Obviously there have to be two people who speak perfect French -Wells replied, somewhat less enthusiastic.

-He will be one of them -said Bogart, pointing to Picasso- and the other must be Monet; there is no one else who speaks French like them.

-Do not you think -said Monet- that I'm old enough to pretend to be an active policeman?.

-My experience with makeup for the cinema will do the miracle. I'll turn him into an attractive fifty-year-old detective. Wells and I will be agents of the British Secret Service who have come to make sure the execution is carried out. Nobody will suspect us because we do not know French.

-But, when do you think about rescuing the girl?

-It will be tomorrow, right here, in the dungeons of the courthouse.

The hours that preceded this risky mission were intense for all. Picasso was in charge of looking for police uniforms among his friends, while Monet solved in a clandestine printing press the preparation of the appropriate documents. Bogart and Wells, on the other hand, were already plotting on paper the situation of the firing squad, the public, the security measures and the route that Mata-Hari would take to where the judge who would speak to the crowd was waiting for her. With all these information present, they were clear that the only possibility of rescuing her while she was in the cells. At night, the four friends made a thorough check of the place, basically the courthouse door and the exact location of the dungeons. They already knew that the execution would take place at nine in the morning and it was expected that thousands of people would cheer on the execution. That is why, that night they hardly slept, while hundreds of questions and fears passed through their minds. Bogart still wondered what he was doing there, in the France of the beginning of the century, trying to rescue from death a beautiful girl with whom he had not even intimated. He analyzed his role as a hero in the movies, hard and skillful handling pistols and women, without understanding how reality could be so different from fiction. Now the danger of death was certain and possibly imminent, while thousands of miles away, in the United States, a wife awaited him with whom he had not even celebrated the wedding night. He looked at HG Wells, a writer with more fantasy in his mind than a child, whom he had considered a madman, although now he saw him as an idealist determined to correct injustices. And in the next room two fans of the brush and the charcoal, teacher and student, trying to change the placid life of artists for the members of a strange political resistance, since they went against their own people.

-When I wake up from this,-said Bogart, in dreams- I will not drink a drop of alcohol again. It has upset my brain.

- (Wells, half-awake) What are you saying?

-Nothing, that I would like to drink a good Scotch or a French cognac.

The next morning, two militants of the French Communist Party brought the police suits they had requested, plus the false documentation for all. Quickly, they put on their suits and checked the forged documents, which mentioned their status as special members of the French and English security services. Bogart, helped by the pictorial gifts of Picasso, elaborated with watercolor and oil a perfect make-up for the face of Monet, who now showed himself as a brave policeman.

They quickly went to the Palace of Justice and there, without hesitation, to the entrance of the dungeons. An iron gate and two armed sentries stopped them.

- You cannot pass; this area is restricted until tomorrow.

- (Picasso, very serene) We bring an order signed by the Intelligence Service which says we have to drive the spy Mata-Hari back to the judge. Important documents have been found in her home that compromise very prominent legal personalities and she should be questioned about it.

The senior sentry picked up the note, looked at it once, handed it to his assistant, and in a firm voice said:

-We have strict orders that no one should approach the prisoner, except with an order signed by the Head of Government himself. Its execution will not be delayed under any circumstances.

-These documents give us maximum authority -Monet replied energetically- and I insist that this woman must be interrogated again before she dies. We are accompanied by two members of the

British Secret Services and if you oppose it will be created an international conflict.

The sentry looked at Wells and Bogart, went over the documents explaining Mata-Hari's transfer order to the judge, and asked Wells to show him his credentials. When he checked it out, he asked Bogart for the same documents and asked him:

-Who is your immediate boss? I must call him by telegraph to confirm your identity.

The request left everyone stunned, essentially because Bogart did not understand a word of the French language. His passivity alerted the sentry, who went to his companion to warn the sergeant on duty. His intentions seemed extremely worrying to everyone.

-Wait! -interrupted Picasso- Don't you realize they don't know French? I will speak to them in English so that they can answer your request.

The conversation he had with Wells and Bogart, of course, had nothing to do with the sentinel's pretensions, but his ignorance of the English language gave them total impunity. In a subtle way and without making gestures that could instill suspicion, he indicated that the French sentry was beginning to suspect and that they should do something quickly or they would all end up like Mata-Hari.

Bogart reassured him and told him that now was his time. With a cynical smile on his lips, the best he had, and pretending to be the most reliable of friends, he moved toward the sentries as he pulled a card out of his raincoat. This card was from a film production company, with a telephone included, but when it was shown to the sentries it seemed to belong to the FBI itself. While the two distrustful Frenchmen looked at the card, trying to decipher what was written in English, Bogart signaled to his companions and the four rushed on the sentries, hitting them in the head. Dismayed and strongly gagged and tied up, they were taken to a nearby back room.

-Well, -said Bogart, taking the reins of the situation- now we must act very quickly. We need to go to the dungeons to get Mata-Hari out of there as soon as possible. We have time until the guard is replaced and we do not know when it will happen.

Quick, but retaining their appearance as special members of the police, the four friends went down into the dark dungeons, until they came across a new police control.

- You cannot entry here! shouted at them. Who has let you in here?

- (Picasso, extremely energetic) We bring express orders from the Intelligence Services to bring the detainee before the judge as soon as possible. She must give a statement before being executed. The sentry at the outside gate has already carried out the appropriate checks. If you want to look at our documents again, here they are.

The policeman carefully read the documents and decided to call the guard post to speak with the sentry. When he picked up the phone he was interrupted abruptly by Picasso.

-Don't waste any more time, stupid! If we take another minute to deliver this woman to the judge, they will take her to the firing squad without being questioned again. You will be responsible for losing information about other spies. I will ask your superiors to form a council of war that will take you to jail for your entire life.

These words, spoken with energy and aggressiveness, plus the sullen look of Bogart, were enough for the suspicious policeman to cross the door, while he began to apologize for his distrust. He quickly opened the door of the dungeon where Mata-Hari was.

- Get out of there, dirty spy! -shouted him- The judge wants to interrogate you again. But don't be misled as nobody will save you from the execution. The square is already crowded with people waiting to see how you die.

More serene than she should be, Mata-Hari picked up her belongings, but not before painting her lips and combing her hair thoroughly.

-I must be beautiful -she argued before everyone's impatience- to speak in front of such an important judge. I will remind him of the pleasant moments we have spent together in your bed when your wife left for the beaches of the Riviera.

This time it was Bogart who grabbed her hard, pulling her out of there quickly. His decision, which for the sentry was interpreted as a sign of the hatred that had it, simplified things and before long everyone was already at the exit door, now without any sentinel.

-We must leave this place as soon as possible -Bogart said- but we need a car. We cannot make any place safe walking.

He looked around and soon found the ideal vehicle parked: a brand new Ford T. He decisively went to the door and putting a handkerchief in one hand hit the front glass until it broke. Once inside it cost him nothing to start the engine, since it was the same model that had led in the movies. And so, once all inside, he hit the accelerator thoroughly without a specific direction.

-Where do we go? Wells asked.

-I do not know -said Bogart- I do not know Paris at all.

While this was happening, Mata-Hari had already been informed by Monet that they were friends who wanted to save her from the shooting, to which she replied:

-I know a perfect place to hide. The church of the Sacred Heart has a suitable crypt for it. That's where the German spies had their station mounted. If they have not found them, they will not find us either.

They quickly crossed the streets of Paris, now almost completely empty by the public shooting that was soon to be held. Its main protagonist, Mata-Hari, smiled looking through the window of the car to the people who hurried to the square where supposedly was going to be executed. Now she was safe, accompanied by four people who had proved more effective than the French policemen who guarded her. Within exactly one hour she should fall dead under the bullets of the firing squad, but now she was safe and guarded by some friends.

All were satisfied except Wells, concerned about the paradoxes of time and its impact on the history of mankind. He did not know the consequences for altering a historical fact, nor what could happen to them if the police stopped them. Accused of spies and accomplices of Mata-Hari's escape, they would surely be shot immediately, something incomprehensible since they did not belong to that time or place. Bogart had yet to become a popular film actor and he still had many trips to make in time. If they died now, who were the ones in 1938?

Without finding an answer to his questions, he looked at his watch and realized something even more terrible: it was about time that the energy of the time machine would be finished and when this happened they would go back in time abruptly. If it happened while Bogart was driving the car, they would probably crash when they ran out driver and it is possible that all their friends died, while Bogart and Wells returned safely to their time.

-Bogart! He said nervously. Stop the car quickly. Do it!

His tone of voice left no doubt about the need to stop and park it in a discreet place, Bogart waited for Wells' explanation.

-Wait a moment here -he said to his companions. My friend and I have to speak urgently alone.

Both got out of the car and while Bogart was questioning Wells, trying to guess what was happening; the three occupants of the car spoke among themselves scared by the event. The sudden stop of the car and the departure of our friends to speak alone, were not the best omen for those escaping from the police. Distrusting them, especially because of Bogart's lack of sympathy for the Communists, and without waiting for an answer, Picasso, Monet, and Mata-Hari hurried out of the car, running down the street to escape from Bogart and Wells, whom they already assumed to be members of the American secret services. If they wanted to capture them they should chase them running faster than them.

But Wells tried to explain to Bogart that they were about to return to his time and that is why he did not notice the escape of his, until now, friends. At that moment, a dim light enveloped them and they were immediately inside the Wells time machine, again in the year 1938. The danger for them had passed.

A few minutes later, Mata-Hari was arrested by the Paris police while trying to enter the Sacred Heart church. Gone were Monet and Picasso, after she escaped from them, suspecting that they were also fascists serving Germany. Her mistrust had led her to commit an error and be imprisoned again, while they had managed to get safe by taking refuge in their attic of Montmartre.

And so, a large crowd, concentrated in Paris on the morning of October 15, 1917, saw Mata-Hari for the last time, now in a simple but elegant dress, in front of the firing squad. She refused twice to have her eyes bandaged and her hands tied behind her back, and she sent a kiss to the firing squad before they pulled the trigger. They say that one of the soldiers, moved by this kiss, and feeling sorry for having to shoot the fatal bullet, fainted right there. Fate had not been altered.

CHAPTER 9

A DISCONCERTING RETURN AND AN INCREDIBLE ENCOUNTER

Stunned, not so much by the trip as by the emotions of the adventure, Wells and Bogart were a few minutes without talking, trying to relive even the most exciting moments of the trip. Bogart immediately ordered a cigarette and a glass of whiskey, while Wells began to take notes and check the elapsed time.

The wristwatch made it clear that this time they had been in the past for more than three days, but the relentless cuckoo clock in his library, as well as the newspaper of the day, indicated that they were still on the same day and time as before embarking on the journey in time. Everything remained the same and it was possible that they had not aged another second.

-Are you sure, my friend Wells -Bogart asked- that it was not all a dream or a hypnotic trance produced by this devilish machine of yours?

-It is difficult for two people to share the same dream, especially simultaneously. In addition, there is an irrefutable proof and they are our wristwatches. If you check yours, you will see that it marks a different time and date than everyone else in this house, an unequivocal sign that there are certainly two parallel universes in which we are moving. First, when we travel to the past, time goes on its course, the same as history. Second, there are also advances in time, but not for us, since we are not in this moment or in this dimension.

- I think that I will leave doubts when I return to my house and see the reception of my wife. (Smiling) If I find her sleeping with another man and throwing me out of the house, your theory is sure to be a solemn nonsense. It could also have happened that here two hundred years have passed and I no longer have family or friends and possibly my house has been demolished to build luxury apartments.

-If this is the case, do not worry, since at least you will already know your destiny and you will know if your presence in the cinema has left a mark. In addition, we will always have Paris.

-I like that phrase; I may include it in one of my films.

Bogart left go back to his wedding party, if it was still on, while Wells noted in his diary all the details of the fabulous journey into the past. Simultaneously, he was already beginning to make plans for his next adventure, trying to find a place or people important enough to make the trip worthwhile. I was not sure if the best thing was to limit myself to being a mere spectator of contemporary history, without taking part in any event, or trying, once again, to modify the historical facts for the good of Humanity. His failed attempt to rescue Mata-Hari from his cruel fate had left him mournful, although he was convinced that only the inopportune return to his time was the cause of failure.

But other doubts assailed him and worried him, especially about the possibility of dying on one of those trips, or when he had the opportunity to be face to face with himself or his family. He did not know what changes could be made in his current life if something of this happened, since the science books did not even hypothetically contemplate that possibility.

Confused in relation to what he had narrated in his novel "The Time Machine", so different from what had actually happened to him, he came up with the idea of writing a second part, now traveling to the past, but faithfully counting all his experiences I knew that at least millions of readers would enjoy and vibrate with emotion for these trips to the past, although they would always be considered pure fiction. Sad destiny for a person who had invented the most amazing machine of all times, but could not show it publicly or gain fame and prestige for it. Even his first mate, Humphrey Bogart, doubted it would have been real and probably could not even count on him for another trip. Once in the loving arms of his wife and with several films about to shoot, surely would not question a new trip. He needed, then, another companion of travels.

His daze led him to wander the streets of New York, waiting for some event to tell him what his path should be from this moment. He was sure that the trip could not be done alone and it did not interest him either, since he emotionally wanted to share the experience and needed witnesses, even if they were as incredulous as Bogart. Sitting on a bench, he contemplated the people passing by, until his eyes settled on a movie theater that was almost in front of him. There they were projecting the film "Room Service", by the Marx Brothers, comedians who he had been fan of since he saw "The Cocoanuts". It was not a bad idea to get distracted a little until the ideas were clearer in his mind.

He chose a rear seat, away from the audience, and attended relaxed to the screening of the film, now well advanced. However, his mind could not concentrate, not so much because his imagination flew frequently from there to his experiences in Paris, but because just behind him were sitting two spectators who liked to express their opinion aloud.

-This argument is all over the place -said one- and it seems only an excuse to introduce the jokes.

-At least they are not as bad as the ones you write -his companion replied.

- True, they are so bad that I have thought to stop writing jokes and work preparing Treasury citations. So at least people would read them.

-Wow! Almost without intending it, something funny has come up.

-But it is true. I am convinced that the Treasury Department is where I have the most admirers. Everyone wants an autograph of me in a check.

-If you at least pay your taxes from time to time ...

-I am under pressure and I even dream of foreclosures and citations. The other day I went to eat at a luxury restaurant and they put me crab, but I did not eat it just in case it was a disguised Treasury inspector.

-You should have chosen another profession, so you would get to eat the crabs without problems.

-Look, I've always wanted to be a doctor, mostly to have nice nurses around me, but you know that our mother took that idea away from my head. She said it was something evil, especially if I was in gynecology.

-Now I understand your interest in playing doctor roles in movies.

-Exactly, but in this film you can see the Machiavellian hand of Zeppo in the script and he has not let me perform any of my favorite anatomical explorations. I am convinced that this is why the film will be a total failure.

The conversation left no room for doubt about its protagonists and Wells was convinced that behind him were at least two of the Marx Brothers. Indeed, and although less recognizable than with his usual costumes from the movies, there were Groucho and Harpo Marx in person.

- Hey, you! Groucho shouted to Wells. Do I have monkeys on my face? At least I give them peanuts from time to time and I do not stop looking at them without saying a word.

- (Wells, stunned by the answer) Excuse me, I thought that ...

-Fascinating. Now tell me in more detail.

-I was saying that...

- I do not understand it. Repeat it

- (Rising nervously) Okay, I'm leaving, I did not want to bother you, it's just that...

- Wait, you cannot stand us up now. If you do you will have to pass over my body. Thinking better, if you leave I'll keep watching this horrible movie and I'll let you come to my funeral another day when I am not there.

Wells rushes out of the room, but in the hall he is gently stopped by Groucho, who outlining the best of his smiles, says:

-Forgive me, it was a joke. I only discuss 3 to 4 in the afternoon and so the rest of the day seems wonderful. (Extending his hand) I am

Groucho Marx and this mouse without cheese that is next to me is my brother Harpo.

-I must confess that for a moment I thought they were really angry - he said, still stunned.

- It bothers us a lot that they confuse us with the Marx Brothers. Harpo, for example, is always confused with Harpo and that is demeaning to him.

-But, are you or are you not the Marx Brothers?

-The truth is that -Groucho replied, taking a breath- when I was born, I wanted to be called Robinson, but my parents were faster than me and they called me Julius. Groucho's thing was my mother's fault and she thought that they would confuse me with one of the Marx Brothers and we would have more work. Poor woman! she was an unhappy woman; She died without being able to go to the toilet before.

-And you, Mr. Harpo -asked Wells, now more relaxed- how have you managed to maintain the myth that you are dumb?" Personally I have always believed that it was true.

- (Groucho, without letting his brother speak) this brother of mine is foolish like a fox, a character without soul or depth, a man admirably simple. One day he forgot the script during a play and continued to act without uttering a word. They applauded him so much, for the first time, that he decided to continue like this all his life. And who are you?

- My name is H. G. Wells.

- Sure, that's why his face reminded me of you! I know a writer who is just like you and who is called like you. Well, it has no merit to look at me like that, but I still insist that there is a great similarity between H. G. Wells and you. How did he say his name was?

-I'm still H. G. Wells.

-Well, as after having been introduced we are still perfect strangers I would like to invite you to my house, but my wife has threatened to reconcile with me if I do.

-We can go to a restaurant.

-Great! Although I want to warn you that whenever I go out to eat I go to the same restaurant. They already know me and they put me near the kitchen door and instead of napkins they bring me an apron. Also, to save they give me spaghetti with anorexia.

-If you prefer, my house is close and I will be happy to invite you to dinner.

- (Harpo, for the first time) If you forgive me, I cannot go with you, I have to meet a friend.

-Listen to my brother-said Groucho. The one time he talks and he intends to make me jealous with his flirting. Anyway, it will not hurt to go out with that girl, because you are more depressed than a mountaineer in the desert. Go and have a good time, but I recommend that if you want to go home early you should forget your wallet on the piano.

-And you Mr. Groucho -Wells said politely- do you also have some commitment with a friend you can bring her to my house. That is all right with me.

- You are cheeky, but unfortunately, I do not have anyone who wants to take my hat off with bites. Yes, I know, I do not even wear a hat, but it does not need to be so impertinent. The truth is that I realized that I no longer good at flirting as before when one day I opened the mailbox and only picked up propaganda; I used to find colored panties. Well, I don't want to listen any more. Let's go!

During the short trip to the house of Wells, Groucho did not stop telling jokes, although there was a moment in which he regained his breath to ask about his novels and confess he loved them.

-The one I liked the most was "Around the World in Eighty Days," he said.

- But that was written by Jules Verne and I am H. G. Wells.

- That is why I thought that your face was familiar to me.

- Do you realize that you have not stopped talking since we left the cinema?

-Since we entered the cinema, friend Wells, since we entered the cinema. My mother told me it was because I had swallowed a phonograph needle.

Wells now wondered if Groucho's choice as a new companion in his time travel would have been successful. He had not yet heard a word or serious comment from that man and was beginning to think that to put him squarely in the story, with the dangers that this would entail, could cause at least a chaos impossible to decipher later by historians and biographers. He wanted that each trip was assisted by a different personality, so that he would have better opportunity to evaluate the events and the usefulness of his time machine, but he began to consider Groucho as a bad option.

-Groucho -Wells asked- are you not able of saying two words together without making a joke? Is there anything in your life that deserves to be serious?

-Impossible. A sense of humor is what helps us endure the stupidity of being alive. How do you explain our desire to stay in our mother for nine months and to have to make so many efforts to get us out? It is obvious that we do not want to be born and that's why we cry to when a stupid doctor pulls us on the head to take us outside.

-But would you like to do something transcendental in life?

- You mean to be able to buy a big car for one dollar or to get to dance with a cow? Both things I have already tried again and again and if you look closely at my face you will know the results. I have also tried to make the tiger jump from the ceiling of a built-in wardrobe, but it has been useless. I know my limitations.

-Try to get serious for once -Wells insisted, arming himself with patience- I'm talking about something like taking a trip to an unknown world, saving Humanity from a disaster or ...

- (interrupts him) Or get to find out what is the trick that women have to seduce. Well, actually, we all know where their trick is, but sometimes I prefer to be ignorant so they can show it to me.

- Please, be serious once!

-The last time I did it was when I wrote a very emotional letter to a friend on the day of her funeral. I told her that I expected her to remain as beautiful as ever and that I wanted to see her very soon.

-I see it's difficult to make you stop joking. Come with me, I want to show you something that might erase that smile from your mouth.

-Where are you taking me? You should know that I have the same interest in accompanying you as in washing in a bidet full of piranhas.

- To the basement of my house.

- Do you know the positive side when the basement floods? (Without waiting for an answer) That we can go fishing without being fined. Listen! This is darker than Dracula's shadow.

CHAPTER 10

WALL STREET

When Wells turned on the lights that illuminated the time machine, showing the strangest artifact Groucho had ever seen, there was silence for a few seconds, something that at least relieved Wells' incipient headache. Groucho straightened, possibly for the first time in his life, scanned the machine, took off his glasses twice and placing his mustache said:

- This is so strange that right now I do not know whether to believe what my eyes see or the nonsense that you have said about time travel. Anyway, I prefer to be quiet than to seem foolish with my questions and manifest my ignorance.

- Do not have interest in knowing what is this device?

-I think it's a wonderful idea.

-But ... I have not yet explained what it is and what it is for.

-Well, it still looks wonderful.

- (Trying to be forceful) This is a time machine, with it we can travel to the past.

-Oh! He said as he walked up and down.

- I have already made several successful trips and I would like you to join me now. My last partner was the actor Humphrey Bogart, but his recent marriage prevents him from traveling with me again.

- Do you know something? Marriage is something strange. For example: I always thought that my niece was so stupid that she would end up marrying a horse. Last month she confirmed that this was true and now they are both running at the racecourse.

- Please, friend, I'm trying that you take me seriously! I do not want to make a joke. This is truly a time machine and it works perfectly. I wish I could prove it to you.

-And could we escape from the tax inspectors on gray suit? If so, where should we get the ticket for this trip? All right, all right. When do we start?

- Wait, wait, we have not decided yet where to go.

-Let's go anywhere you do not have to listen to opera. Every time I have to go to the opera I ask the taxi driver to go slowly. I feel pretty bad that we arrive before the function has finished.

-I think I'll have to make the decision myself. What do you think if we travel to the year 1929, a couple of days before the collapse of Wall Street?

-Well, but I think my brother Harpo is not going to like the idea.

-Why?

- That day I accompanied his wife home and has not yet returned. I told him that I had no reason to be worried about this absence, but when his third son was born and his wife did not even come to give birth, he began to suspect that something was not right.

Finally sketching a smile at the comic delirium of Groucho Marx, Wells prepared the time machine properly by putting a photograph of the New York Stock Exchange building, in whose vicinity hundreds of people were worried about their savings. He turned on the power generator and quickly X-rays hit the photo. Afterwards, they passed through the bodies of the two friends and the image merged perfectly into the cathode ray tube, taking them back on a quick journey through history.

When they arrived, the commotion of the people concentrated in the street was intense, since the news that came from the inside were extremely confusing. The price of the shares rose and fell scandalously every minute, while the small savers went from poverty to wealth with the same ease. With most of the stocks overvalued because of the great economic growth of the postwar period, the Americans had been fooled by the stockbrokers and asked the banks for loans to buy the shares they considered safe. At that time, more than a million people were indebted to the banks and could not pay their loans due to the large fluctuation of the shares.

When Wells and Groucho appeared abruptly in the middle of the shouting, no one paid them any attention.

-We must have traveled first class- Groucho protested. This trip has made me a little dizzy.

-Don't worry, the effects of the radiation will pass soon. Now it is important that we plan our available time well, since the machine will only work for three days. Where do you think we go in the first place?

-I would like to visit my wife to see if it is true that she cheats on me with that great man called Groucho Marx. They told me it's a beast making love.

-It should take this jump in time more seriously. My advice is to not intervene in your own destiny; the consequences are unpredictable.

-Oh, don't worry about that! My wife has decided to take years off every birthday and if I'm lucky soon we will not even be married and I'll be able to visit her at her baptism. It will be like visiting my granddaughter.

- Wait a little, you have to meditate the consequences of your actions and make good use of this trip in time. I think the first thing is to sell all our shares, now that they still have some value. Within two days, just on October 24, more than 13 million shares will go on sale and none will be worth more than a penny. We have to go to the bank right now so they can sell them at the best price.

The stock market transaction was not a problem for either of them, since it was enough with their personal identification to sell all their shares and that the resulting money was automatically deposited in their current accounts.

-Now that I remember...! Groucho said abruptly as he left the bank. Tomorrow is the day my mother died and at that moment I could not be by her side. I would like to go to my house to be present.

-You know it's not wise to see your family or anyone you know. Keep in mind that we have traveled nine years into the past and your entire family will be ten years younger, including you.

-Thanks for the compliment.

-You did not understand me. What do you think would happen if your family saw you now, suddenly aged nine years?

- But you have not told me that I will be nine years younger?

-I was referring to your other self, the one who lives now in 1929. You remain the same because you belong to 1938.

-I'm glad you explain it to me with that clarity because now I know that I'm not Groucho Marx the young man, but Groucho Marx the old man. Anyway, if I look in the mirror I'm sure I'll look like Groucho Marx and I think there will be a great resemblance between the two. I am also sure that if I go to my wife's house she will not notice the difference, unless she is with me in bed. I have an idea: why don't you go to my house to see if my wife is cheating on me?

- (Irritated) If I have to be honest, I must admit that I should never have brought you with me to this trip in time. You daze me with your jokes.

- Do you know why I married Ruth?

-I'm afraid you'll tell me even if I'm not interested, so...

-One day she made me drink champagne in one of her shoes. She was size 38 and when I was half way I looked her in the eyes and I fell in love with her. Her eyes shone like my blue pants when they're dirty. There was a time when instead of eyes I saw whales and the champagne already had an intense taste of rotten herring. It was a wonderful night.

- (Clearly dizzy) It's okay, you win. We will go to see your family.

But when they finally arrived, trying to remain hidden from the neighbors, a coffin carried on the shoulders of some people indicated without a doubt that they had arrived late. His mother was already on her last trip, now more acclaimed than during all her previous life as an actress. Around him were the five Marx brothers, numerous relatives from all American states, the press and dozens of fans who had come with the desire to be close to the already popular Marx Brothers.

Groucho tried to get closer, but Wells' strong hand holding him made him think. His countenance went from initial gloom to show his usual scathing irony.

-Look, they are my brothers. Chico is the one who looks like a horse and who seems to hurt his feet, and Harpo who is eating the whole tray of cakes. Who I don't know is that handsome young man who looks like the Prince of Wales.

- Is it possible that you do not recognize yourself?

-What? What you said is an insult! If you were not older than me I would hit you for what you just said.

-But if I'm bigger than you...

-So you could beat me.

-Mr. Marx -Wells replied, again upset -you are forcing me to talk the same nonsense as you. I was hoping that attending the death of your mother again would made you more serious, but I see that you are incorrigible.

-It would be the first time in life that someone wept twice at the same funeral, especially if they were celebrated nine years apart.

-I believe that the time has come for us to do something more useful for Humanity than to continue telling jokes and nonsense. The first thing is to leave this place, since they can recognize us.

-Well, I propose that we go to eat to an Italian restaurant. Do you know that my brother Chico was not Italian? Well, neither am I and

I have never boasted of it, but at least I know how to make myself understood in perfect Italian. I know four key words to move without problems through the center of Rome: "Kiss me, fast", "Help, I've been bitten by a snake!", "I have to feed my cat" and "Oh, another fine! "

-Okay, I give up -answered Wells, discouraged. We're going to eat at an Italian restaurant.

-I hope it is not one of those in which the waiter has the habit of passing the bill when finished eating.

Little Italy was the place where most of the Italian immigrants lived and its aroma was noticeable even in the streets. Attached to the emblem Chinatown, both ways of life managed to coexist without problems until the arrival of the gangsters seriously complicated their existence. The chosen restaurant was Umberto's Clam House, located on Hester Street, a place famous for its exquisite seafood.

-Groucho, don't you think this place is too expensive for us?

-Not for me; maybe for you as the one who will pay. Anyway, we'll sit close to the exit just in case. Don't forget about "women and children first"; Sometimes I feel like a baby.

-I hope the coins of our time have been coined long ago and are equally valid now.

-You have to trust people, friend Wells, you have a big family wanting to be useful.

- From that point of view it does not seem such a bad idea to me.

-Well forget them and eat those raviolis with tomato, you don't expect that besides you paying the bill I will have to eat your food too.

CHAPTER 11

AL CAPONE

Everything seemed to proceed normally until H. G. Wells began to think that precisely the presence of Groucho Marx could bring him greater benefits than planned. His character and his point of view to judge the events provided a vision of the history of the new and comforting Humanity. With a margin still of two days to be able to carry out actions and visits to New York, before the time machine made them return to their time, they could try to warn the world of possible misfortunes and alert them to the danger posed by the advance to power of some political leaders.

He could warn them of the plundering of the Jews residing in Germany that would deprive them of all their rights and property, or of the disastrous march of Mao Zedong to the province of Shaanxi that would kill 90,000 men. He also knew about the future invasion of Abyssinia by Italy, the disaster of the Hindenburg airship in which 37 people died because of sabotage, and the global consequences of the Great Depression. But his problem was the same as in the other trips, since it would not do him any good to go to one of the New York newspapers and explain that thanks to his time machine he knew the destiny of Humanity for the next nine years. Not even his well-earned prestige as a fiction writer could provide him with a minimum of credibility.

All these thoughts were interrupted abruptly by the entrance to the restaurant of four men armed with Thompson machine guns.

-Everybody on the floor! This is a robbery!

That energetic warning should be something habitual in that area, since the waiters first and later the clients, all were thrown to the ground immediately without shouting or yells of protest. The four thugs, dressed so impeccably that they looked like bankers, fired some shots at the ceiling and the shelves, while a fifth appeared on the scene carrying on his shoulders a luxurious wool coat. Wells and Groucho, on the other hand, had not yet had time to react and they were still sitting watching the events with amazement. The newcomer addressed them.

-I see that these two gentlemen do not understand our language. Maybe they better understand my Tommy's sound -he said, pointing to his machine gun.

-Do not wait! -Wells shouted.

It was useless. The machine gun aimed directly at his eyes, while the gangster smiled. The trigger moved, but fortunately the weapon jammed and that was when Groucho dared to plead for his life, or at least that was what Wells believed.

-"Sir," he said, rising ceremoniously. You should know that you are very lucky to be in front of two important persons like us. Don't think that we are here to taste the exquisite Italian dishes, but to assure you and your friends that within a very short time you will have spent five minutes, not one more, not one less. Let's say ... within 300 seconds.

Not only the bully was speechless with this phrase of Groucho, but the whole restaurant was plunged into a mental state close to stupor. No one was able to find out what he had meant, not even if it was a larval threat or a code word. The silence that followed was increasingly tense, while none dared to move a single finger. At that moment and just when everyone expected a brutal response from the gangster, a loud laugh came out of his mouth adorned with a large amount of saliva. Within seconds the whole restaurant was laughing non-stop, some for chanting their partner and others to prevent the machine guns from spitting their bullets again.

- For the sainted Madonna, I had never heard such nonsense! Said the thug satisfied. Who are you?

-Gentlemen, and forgive me for calling you that, until a minute ago it was Groucho Marx, but now I look more like a piece of melted butter. Or a piece of flan just when I fell in the crotch. Choose what you like, but give me back the change.

The attitude of the gangster, whom the reader must have already identified as Al Capone, changed abruptly and we could even say that he was very friendly.

-And how can someone who has such a ridiculous name be able to say such a funny phrase?

-If you give me two bucks I will tell you the secret. Even better.. if you let us go, I'll send you a telegram asking you for three hundred dollars to pay the landlord.

-As my name is Al Capone -he said with a laugh - I shot this guy before he killed me with laughter. And this grandfather, who is at your side so pale, is your father?

Wells got up too and something calmer than a moment ago he held out his hand to the gangster, obviously without finding an answer on his part. Nervous and extremely frightened at the unkind response, he looked at Groucho, demanding immediate help.

-Oh, do not worry about my friend! Groucho said, putting himself now in the middle of the two. He actually stayed like that, speechless, when he saw the price list of this restaurant. I would advise you, Mr. Bully with a machine gun, to go to another place where we can be served a pig in a poke, or even better, a fishbone to give it to my cat.

-Before I leave, I have a job to do here -he said as he addressed the owner of the store and said loudly. If you do not want to take a car ride with me and end up with a bullet lodged in your stomach, tomorrow you will have to pay us $ 10,000 for the protection we offer you. And now you and I, impertinent mustachioed, we are going to go to my house to have some whiskeys. Your dumb friend can come with us.

Exiting as quickly as they entered, the thugs climbed into a huge car with tinted windows and embrasures to fire from within, and made their way quickly to an unknown place on the outskirts of the city.

-I should have blindfolded them so they would not know where my lair is -Capone said- but since I'm going to kill them anyway, there's no problem with me getting caught. Now you should feel fortunate to be still alive and to enjoy my hospitality, since I am not used to having so much patience.

-Mr. Capone ...- the driver said softly.

- (Screaming) Capone, my name is Al Capone! If you forget it again, I'll blow that stupid brain you have in your head.

-Excuse me, Mr. Al Capone, I will not forget it. I wanted to tell you that I know the guy with the mustache. I've seen him work in the cinema with his brothers. He's a very good comedian and I think we could ask for a good ransom for him.

-Now I understand his jokes! So you are a comedian who works in the cinema? And the future dead beside him, who is it?

The answer never arrived since a police siren sounded powerful behind them, while new cars appeared on all sides. Soon the shots began to sound and an amazing race through the streets of the suburbs of New York took place. But Al Capone's Cadillac was not exactly any vehicle, and its armored body perfectly resisted bullet impacts, while the powerful eight-cylinder engine was capable of leaving behind the ineffective police cars. The persecution began to complicate when new police vehicles joined the first and soon the bullet impacts began to resonate with force, at first without penetrating and little by little managing to enter the weakest areas. And one of these shots hit the driver, who unable to control the car accurately could not prevent it from crashing hard against the shop window. Fortunately, the robust and well-designed cabin of the car prevented its occupants from suffering any damage and although somewhat resentful of the impact, they all left unharmed to the street, just when at least a dozen policemen pointed their weapons at them.

- Mr. Capone! -announced one of the police officers-, it's about time you went back to sleep at Alcatraz. There a well-fluffy bed, your usual newspaper and a splendid grate await for you so that you will not forget us in many years.

-My name is Al Capone! Alfonso Capone! And if you forget again, your wife will be a widow very soon," he said angrily.

-You should be nicer in front of a well-armed policeman. You are not in a position to demand anything. You and your friends are going to come with me to a solid cell so that you can meditate about your future for a long time.

When more than a dozen policemen surrounded them, Wells and Marx decided that the time was right to let them know of their kidnapping status, but a few violent shoves, plus some unintentional blows with the truncheons, showed them that this was not the most appropriate time for presentations. A few minutes later, a cellular car, properly armored, served as a vehicle for everyone, now heading directly to the district police station.

On the way Wells examined his head, now adorned with a modest bump, and looked through his pockets for a credential that would allow him to explain to the police his status as an English tourist. But something must have happened during the accident, since nothing was found and a chill ran through his body when he imagined trying to give a plausible explanation in the police station about his presence in Al Capone's car. His left ankle also hurt and for a few minutes he remained in deep meditation, until a groan from Groucho made him see that his friend was also hurt.

-My body is now worse than a deflated balloon -he said when he noticed Wells looking at him. Except for the nose I would change everything for that of a beautiful woman, so at least I would like myself.

- Do you have a special appreciation for your nose?

-Not at all, but at least on my nose those policemen cannot put me in a pair of handcuffs.

-I see that even though we are in a good mess, you still keep your desire to joke.

-My proposal is that we go out and ask for a taxi. If we do not get it we can try to get angry, although we could also get angry now and ask for the taxi later. If the cops think it's too early for the turn of anger, we can wait a minute longer.

The energetic braking of the police van indicated that they had reached their destination, the darkest police station in the entire city.

There, heavily escorted by the police, all the detainees entered directly to the premises where the criminals were usually interrogated. Groucho and Wells were separated from the group of gangsters and taken to another room, even more gloomy, but in which there were at least chairs, a table and a giant mirror through which they would be observed by other detectives. Groucho signaled to Wells warning him to let him talk to them.

"Well -the first detective began- Now you are going to explain to me how Capone managed to escape from Alcatraz and get to New York without being arrested.

- (Groucho, taking the reins) Oh, do not worry, we will sing everything you want since we are the orchestra of the party. Actually, we should have arrived tomorrow, but my friend Wells decided it was better to arrive a day early in case there was still some dessert on the table.

- What party do you mean?

-It was a dinner with a buffet in which a clown named Schmalhausen should act. Our mission was to arrive as soon as possible to force him to say two jokes in a row and get people to leave soon. I had already threatened diners about this probability and I warned them that if they did not leave he would start his jokes.

-And what did Capone need an orchestra for?

-Really he did not want any orchestra and that's why he hired us, because we charge for no working. We always arrive a day later, when the holidays are over and so people do not continue to drink champagne.

-I see -the policeman continued, enjoying the dialogue- And how much was he going to pay for not working?"

- One hundred dollars an hour.

-It's a bit expensive and I think it would be cheaper for Capone to make you work.

-Well, for greedy people we only rehearse and we make a special price. Just two hundred dollars an hour.

-But if you do not work, what do they have to rehearse?

-Well, the things that you have to rehearse. My brother Harpo, for example, rehearses how to put women horizontally in two seconds. If he lends me his wife for a moment I will explain it to you in detail.

-I think it would be better if you do not pay them for rehearsing. Do they have a fee for not playing or rehearsing?

-You could not afford the payment. You should know that if we do not rehearse we do not work and if we do not work our price increases, although we can reach an agreement.

- (Holding back the laughter) Well, I'd like to see how we can come to an agreement.

-You see: yesterday we were not here. He remembers?

-Oh, yes I remember it!

- Then you owe me three hundred dollars already.

-I get it. Yesterday you did not come and I owe you three hundred dollars. It seems reasonable, but I find it cheap.

-I knew you would lose with this business. By the way, could we not go for a walk outside, on the terrace or better down the street?

- Now, you would like to walk somewhere else now, isn't it?

-No sir, that would not be gentlemen's and I do not consider you as such. Well, are we going or do you prefer that I say "see you later darling"?

- (Exiting the jocular talk) Do you know, mustachioed friend, that you are accused of belonging to the band of Al Capone and that you will be at least five years in prison? But you should be happy about it, because at Alcatraz you will find opportunities to keep telling bad jokes.

It is the most nauseating proposal that I have been made in my life. Although thinking about it, the worst was when the justice of peace asked me if I wanted to marry my wife.

-And you -he said to Wells- also want to tell me some jokes before I put you in jail?

-What I would want is for you to call my embassy to clarify our situation -he answered, less jovial than Groucho. I am an English citizen who was eating quietly in that Italian restaurant until those mobsters arrived firing with their machine guns.

-You are as bad lying as your friend telling jokes Do you have any identification?

-I've lost mine during the fray -Wells said ruefully. Even so, I must mention that I am a popular writer called H. G. Wells and that this mustachioed friend, as you derisively call him, is the actor Groucho Marx, one of the best comedians in the world.

-I understand - the policeman said sarcastically- and that's why you decided to take a ride in Al Capone's car, maybe to get to know the suburbs or to find a new argument for your films. Am I right?

-As true, -Groucho said- as that I enrolled once at the University of Basar.

-I see that you are also fond of big lies, since that is a girls' college.

-I discovered it in the third year, and that was because it occurred to me to go to the solarium one day.

-Well, since you do not intend to clarify your relationship with Capone, you will stay here until I can move you to Alcatraz prison. Meanwhile, I will try to find out your true identities.

When the door of the dungeon closed tightly, Wells and Groucho began to realize that their situation was more delicate than it appeared. Both knew that there was no rational way to prove they were not members of the gangster's gang, with both the absence of personal documents and the verbal incongruity of Groucho who, in addition, did not have more documents than a union card. of film actors, too little for a policeman so incredulous.

Soon the night came and with it the hopes that someone could set them free. All reasoning led to the same conclusion: being two travelers in time no one knew of their existence in that dungeon, and no one could miss them, especially now, in the past. Moreover, if Groucho insisted on proving his true identity, his true self would soon appear, the Groucho Marx of 1929, while he belonged to 1938. If understanding this strange circumstance was difficult for Groucho, with a double nine years younger to whom his mother just died, it would be more complicated to make him understand the policeman in charge of the case. The only viable solution was for Al Capone to free them from this situation by explaining how they got to his car, but now they were both locked in different cells and could not express their desire to him.

CHAPTER 12

ALCATRAZ JAIL

The next morning, the rude voice of a policeman asking them to get up woke them up. Their next destination was the prison of Alcatraz, where they would wait until their trial because as they belonged to an armed gang they would be behind bars for life.

Al Capone had just killed seven members of a rival gang on Valentine's Day and had been required to appear before the Grand Jury on March 12 of that year, but his lawyers managed to cancel that summons thanks to a medical certificate. In that document it was ensured that Al Capone was in Miami, in bed, suffering from pneumonia and could not go to any judicial summons. Meanwhile, numerous false witnesses prepared to elaborate an alibi that would prevent him from being judged. In a few hours, they were able to provide evidence that Al Capone was on a cruise to Nassau on the day of the massacre. But on this occasion his evidence was considered false and on March 27 he had to appear before the Grand Jury, although not only refused to respond to the accusations of the prosecutor, but also insulted all members of the court.

Two months later, and once a fine of $ 5,000 was paid, he was again charged, this time for illegal possession of firearms, being sentenced to one year in prison at Alcatraz, a sentence he never fulfilled since he repeatedly went out buying the guardians. But this time the involuntary presence of Wells and Groucho favored him, since he stated that he was quietly eating in that Italian restaurant with some friends, just when they abruptly burst some individuals firing their machine guns. The rest was equally credible, since they all left the place quickly and escaped quickly in their car. Logically, he could not explain that they were really his hostages, and mentioning them as endearing friends of childhood, his excuse had every chance of being believed.

The arrival to the Rock was on a morning as cold as usually shown in the movies. It was drizzling, there was a mist, the squawking of seagulls was heard, and the waves breaking on the cliffs showed more power than ever. Wells and Groucho, duly handcuffed, were quickly introduced to the premises after crossing a gray and deserted courtyard, being observed through the small windows of the cells by some inmates. Soon they were forced to get naked to be washed with the colder water they had never felt on their skin, they took out several photographs that would remain forever in the police files, and they were given a pair of clothes that they should wear during their stay in jail. And so, they began to live an episode of their lives that could have not even been part of any of their darkest nightmares.

Fortunately, for everyone, life at La Roca was not as disgusting and monotonous as was normally supposed. Like other prisons of this time, Alcatraz allowed certain freedoms for those who respected the rules and did what were asked of them. These freedoms were called "privileges," and for some prisoners they were their only reason for living, and an emotional escape from incarceration at times for life. Some of these privileges included the right to request a lamp or a portion of food in the community restaurant.

Visits were forbidden, though carefully granted to certain prisoners, especially if they had money and friends to bypass the rules. Good conduct allowed them to read the duly censored books and magazines of the island library. Likewise, the prisoner could have the right to correspond with friends and family from abroad, but even the letters were carefully censored and any material that was considered as a threat to the institution was prohibited. For Wells and Groucho these privileges were not only unthinkable, but useless, since their letters could not travel nine years to the future. Their hopes of finding help abroad were nil, as well as getting someone to believe their status as innocent prisoners.

Their first day in that prison was not as unpleasant as they expected and among the authorized amenities were the walks in the courtyard. There you could do anything, if by that we understand walking, sitting on the floor, talking, looking at the clock and again walking or sitting. You could also play cards, but there was a danger of losing everything to the experts or, even worse, not being able to pay the debts incurred in the game. Another option was to look far away at the bustling life of San Francisco, located less than two miles away, something depressing for those who knew they would never leave again. And so, while they were there contemplating the nearby and at the same time distant city, depending on the point of view, they were approached by Al Capone, with an incredible smile.

-Well, well ... my nice friends reunited. I celebrate seeing you in your house. How are you after the accident?

-That question is irrelevant - Groucho answered, more serious than usual. Whether it's good or bad is my business.

-Don't be angry at me, I just want to be nice -replied Al Capone smiling.

-Yes, as a crocodile about to kiss a duck.

-Or a monkey.

- Do not get your family in this matter.

-You start to annoy me with your jokes -the gangster said, twisting his face. You should know that Al Capone cannot be insulted without receiving a visit from my "friends" immediately.

-Don't bother and tell them to leave the visit for later, I'm now sleeping.

- (Spitting his cigar just freshly finished) My insolent friend, you are playing with fire.

-I have a fire insurance.

- (A bit more patient) I have the intention of asking you to join me, to be part of my band. I need people like you who are educated and who can speak without using weapons. I want to show the world that Al Capone is an honest person. If you accept, in less than a week we will all be out of here laughing at the police.

- Working with you must be more dangerous than playing with a machine gun in an elevator. And how much will our fees go up?

-I had thought of 200,000 dollars a year.

- Doesn't it seem too much? I was going to ask for only 600 dollars. Where to sign? I will put the O and Wells the K.

But this business was interrupted abruptly by a group of burly blacks who came threateningly to our friends. Al Capone recognized them immediately - they were irreconcilable enemies - and tried to escape, although an accurate punch in the face stopped him. Meanwhile, the prison guards and the rest of the prisoners began to look elsewhere, aware that a new settling of accounts was coming.

Soon there were already at least six thugs surrounding Capone, Wells and Groucho, all armed with stilettos, punches and iron bars. The gangster had fallen to the ground and while his nose was bleeding abundantly someone was already grabbing his hair, at the same time that a second accomplice brandished a stiletto towards his stomach. Suddenly, a luminous glow flooded the place paralyzing everyone, and Wells and Groucho were wrapped in a beautiful blue light, while they already made their return to the future, to 1938.

The time machine had finished its energy at the most opportune moment and now they were back to their time, safe and sound.

-Caramba! Groucho shouted. "A bit longer and they would have turned us into Gruyère cheese.

- Sometimes I wonder if you are a man or a mouse.

-Place some cheese on the ground and you will see.

Wells tried to follow Groucho's jokes a little, though the weariness of this new journey through time had left him exhausted and sad.

-The truth is that things have been more complicated than desirable. I wanted to show you in a simple way the virtues of my time machine and we were almost killed by Al Capone's rivals.

-Don't worry about it, or feel guilty about the disaster. No one can simultaneously have Einstein's brain and ask to be smiled by the goddess Fortuna. I, for example, have the sagacity of Sherlock Holmes and the beauty of Rodolfo Valentino, but I cannot eat a tuna sandwich without staining my fingers with grease. If luck is not on your side, possibly when you open the gas spigot to commit suicide, Jehovah's Witnesses will knock on the door to give you a talk.

-Yes, I think it was Shakespeare who said that the secret was to be in the right place at the right time.

- That's what I try when I play tennis.

- Would you like to repeat the trip to another place and more quiet time?

-You are able to embark on the Titanic, so you better look for another companion of adventures. I will now go out to the street to throw lascivious glances at pretty girls and I hope that some will be tempted to be raped by my penetrating gaze. Goodbye friend! I must admit that I really liked your book about the war of the worlds; The impossible love between Martians and men was touching. I think I'll read it someday.

That was the last time they both spoke, since from that day they followed very different paths. For Wells the company of Groucho Marx had been sometimes annoying, often unbearable, and sometimes fun, but overall it was a rewarding experience that gave new vigor.

Now he did not know how to continue his experiments and even if he should continue with the idea of looking for new partners. Immersed in doubts about the true usefulness of his time machine, perfect for traveling but useless to solve problems, he tried to find a system so that in his next trip he could contribute something of interest to Humanity. Otherwise, travel to the past to be a mere spectator of events would not provide more benefit than looking at a photograph of the time or a documentary.

At times, Wells was simply compared to a historian who tries to explain more accurately the past events, without having taken an active part in them, a position so comfortable to judge the history that seemed despicable. Destiny could not be something so untouchable, so indelibly written, so that nothing and no one was capable of altering it, not even having a time machine. There had to be a way to be able to be in the past and alter events, without the paradoxes of time producing a world cataclysm.

And in that reasoning was when the phone rang.

Who was on the other side of the line was Orson Welles, his old friend, now more talkative than ever because he had in his power two cinematographic contracts that assured him of being able to demonstrate his great creative capacity. He told him about his many ideas about that film, which he definitely mentioned as "Citizen Kane", and about his desire to go to Spain, a country in which he hoped to find the inspiration needed for all his projects. He also asked, of course, about the results on the time machine, although showing great skepticism about its viability. When H. G. Wells explained the trips he had already made and told him about the many adventures that had taken place, skepticism gave way to total disbelief, since so many days had not passed for him. As much as the inventor tried patiently, he could not convince Welles of the difference between real time and time in the past.

-You, dear friend -Orson Welles accused him mildly- are trying to make me believe that you have already traveled to Paris, that you have been with Mata-Hari, that you have met Al Capone, and that you have been in prison. Alcatraz, and all that in just three days.

-Three days of his time, but I try to explain that when you travel to the past, the present time does not change for a second. Fortunately, I have the endorsement provided by Humphrey Bogart and Groucho Marx, who can explain that everything I have told you is true.

-I must inform you that Mr. Bogart contacted me yesterday and told me about the strange dream he had had. According to his comments, he had had a conversation with you about the possibility of traveling to the past, to the Paris of the beginning of the century, and that between the alcohol he had drunk and his fantastic comments; he had had a terrible nightmare. He said he was persecuted by the Nazis for having rescued Mata-Hari with the help of painters.

-It was not a dream, but a total reality," he replied ruefully. Certainly, we were there thanks to the time machine, just as I have also traveled with Groucho Marx just one day before the collapse of the New York Stock Exchange. I cannot prove to you that everything

I have lived is true, except for the fact that now my savings are safe. You must believe me.

-But don't you even think for a moment that everything is the result of your imagination? Don't you think that actually what you call Time Machine is a device that produces fantastic dreams in a state of hypnosis? You has not managed to bring a single proof of the past to confirm these supposed trips and I think you should separate fantasy from reality. It is logical to be attractive the idea of being able to make trips in time, but when nobody has still confirmed those trips maybe it is because they have never really been made.

-I was thinking- he answered, frankly demoralized- that you had called me to come with me on the next trip, but I see that I will have to do it alone on this occasion.

-Don't be angry at me, Herbert, I'm not trying to take away your dreams or your fantasies. What I want is for you to be realistic and dedicate yourself to continue writing your wonderful novels. Leave the world of hypnotism in the hands of experts. I have recently read that X-rays are a danger to health and I ask you not to continue experimenting with that machine. I prefer to know that you continue to write in your comfortable home, instead of having to visit a dark hospital.

I am grateful that deep down I am worried about my health and my life, although I regret that you do not believe me. Now I would like to rest a little to know where I should direct my next steps.

The conversation was cut off abruptly and if there was any goodbye, it did not pass through the telephone line. Slightly sad by the conversation, Wells sat down in his comfortable big-eared armchair, and looking at a corner of his library he thought about everything that had happened to him until now. His eyes passed fleetingly around the room, while his mind traveled feverishly to dream worlds. And on this tour he saw an archeology magazine dedicated to the great pyramids of Egypt. At some point in his past years he had felt a great interest in the life of the pharaohs and their impressive funerary mausoleums, looking for ideas for a forthcoming novel there. Although he considered himself too old to start a new fiction novel, something crossed his mind at that moment that made him greedily take the magazine.

CHAPTER 13

TUTANKAMON

The article was about the event that occurred on November 26, 1922, in a remote valley of Egypt, when an Egyptologist, Mr. Howard Carter, and the philanthropist Lord Carnarvon, had managed to reach the tomb of Tutankhamun, who died in 1323 a.C. when I was 17 years old. And in the photograph of the magazine were Carter and Carnarvon showing a big triumphant smile in front of the tomb of the mythical pharaoh.

It was the opportunity that Wells was waiting for to make a trip to the past that could finally bring a bit of practicality to his discovery of time travel. Now he would no longer try to improve or modify social events and not even to prevent chilling catastrophes; his next trip would be exclusively for him, for his restless spirit and his desire for knowledge. Gone are their dreams of changing favorably the destiny of Humanity or of seeking the recognition of scientists and the world towards their invention. Linked inevitably to that legion of inventors who see saddened how their great ideas will never see commercial light, he was determined to make the best trip of his life, possibly the last one he could make.

In his library he soon found some information, very brief, about the tomb of Tutankhamun, which was described as KV 62, a small tomb compared to the others but had in its favor the fact of having remained intact for more of 3,000 years. Tutankhamun King or Tutankhamen, son of Akhenaten and Kiya, was only 7 years old when he ascended the throne of Egypt in the year 1333 a.C. and we know that he died very young, at age 17, possibly of pneumonia. His tomb was searched unsuccessfully for hundreds of years in the Western Valley, near that of his grandfather Amenhetep II, a place that subsequently proved to be erroneous.

The entrance to the tomb was buried in the floor of the Valley of the Kings, we do not know if deliberately or perhaps because the land level was formerly lower than at present, especially because of the strong and continuous movements of sand that occur in the desert. Another factor that contributed to its hiding from the Pharaonic treasure thieves was that it was located just in front of KV 9, the tomb of Ramses VI, and now we know that when this tomb was built ruins and earth were unloaded on top of the entrance of the KV 62. No one knew that there was such an important grave underground or if they knew it they never gave it enough archaeological importance. The truth is that the enclave of this tomb was forgotten for years and even a series of huts for the workers of Ramesside were built on it.

The rest of the information was quickly taken up by HG Wells, who soon deposited the photograph of the scientific event on his machine, adjusted the intensity of the current generator to the maximum and started it so that the X-rays could pass through his body and carry him back to the past. In a few seconds, his figure materialized in front of the main entrance of the Egyptian tomb, just as Howard and Carnarvon began to descend the stairs of the main entrance. As they were in front of Wells they could not see their new companion, who with the greatest possible secrecy followed them down the descendants of stairs, now discreetly illuminated by oil lamps.

After removing a pile of rubble, an unequivocal sign that it had already been desecrated, they arrived at a door closed with an oval seal in which the name of Tutankhamun appeared. Both investigators -without perceiving the presence of H. G. Wells behind them-, carefully removed some stones that partially blocked the entrance and entered a dark corridor.

- Do you see anything? Carnarvon asked.

- (Carter, after a hopeful silence) Yes, I see fabulous, incredible things. I think we have found the greatest pharaonic legacy in history. Bring a lamp here.

And it was at this moment, when he turned around to pick up the lamp, when they both saw Wells, who remained motionless behind them, with his eyes wide open to try to see something in the dark.

-But who are you? Howard asked, showing a mixture of stupor and fear.

-Excuse me if I scared you -Wells said- but I have not been able to let you know of my presence before.

-This area is forbidden to tourists -Carnarvon muttered a little more confidently. You have to leave right now or you will be put in jail; and I can assure you that Egyptian prisons are not like ours.

-If you can calm down a bit -Wells continued, while trying to calm them down with his hands- I'll explain the reason for my presence here. (He was already elaborating in his mind a fictional story that was credible by the two archaeologists) I am not a tourist, much less a tomb profaner, I am a professor at the University of Oxford who is trying to find the origin of the Egyptian civilizations.

- Do you have any credentials that endorse your words?

-I'm not here with a scholarship, I'm sorry. I'm just a professor about to retire who wants to leave some philosophical legacy to his students.

-So ... another Englishman looking for emotions -Carnarvon said more calmly. The fact is that your face is familiar to me, although now I do not know where I have seen you. Anyway, sir ... what's your name?

- My name is H. G. Wells.

-Oh God! Howard shouted. Are you certainly H. G. Wells, the writer? I did not know that you were also teaching at the University of Oxford. I thought that fiction writers are not much appreciated among that bunch of pedantic philosophers.

- (Wells, now with his face contracted) Well, I think I cannot continue to keep such a stupid lie with you any longer. I am not here as an Egyptologist, but because of my status as an inventor.

-I do not understand the relationship between the pyramids and inventions.

-Although it may seem incredible to you, and I am sure it will seem to you, I have managed to successfully invent a time machine. I have not appeared here by chance in this grave. This event has been possible thanks to my invention that has allowed me to travel until this day of the year 1922, from my own time in 1938.

-I begin to think that your imagination has no limits, Mr. Wells - Carnarvon said smiling. So a time machine to travel to the past ...

- (Howard, complacent) You do not need to invent such a fantastic excuse to explain your presence in this tomb. It would be enough to have told us that you are collecting material for a new novel and we would have accepted you with equal enthusiasm. The fantasy that you show in your writings does not differ too much from the life of the pharaohs. They had their gods and their immortal life in these pyramids and you, on the other hand, invented the food of the gods to mitigate the hunger of Humanity.

-Well -Carnarvon said impatiently- I think it's about time we start the way into this grave. Between the three of us we will be able to move with greater precision the stones that impede our progress. For my part, since he is here, I do not care if you are a writer or a tourist if you help us in our work. But it seems too much about that time machine -he said- shaking his head as he descended the stairs.

They had barely taken sixteen steps, when they found a sealed door covered with old engravings representing the Valley's guards. Equipped with small beaks and patiently using their hands to extract the limestone rocks that formed the obstacle one by one, they gradually cleared the path. After three hours of work they had managed to make a hole large enough to fit a lamp. Through it they saw what looked like a rather long passageway, at the bottom of which another hermetic seal could be glimpsed.

- I think we have another important obstacle in the background, said Howard. It would be convenient to rest a little before continuing.

- Are not you afraid of being assaulted by grave robbers? Wells asked them.

- Nobody knows that this tomb exists, at least no person from this place. The people here have the conviction that we are looking for pots buried in the sand and will not bother us (hesitating), for the time being. We will have the problem if we find the treasures that we hope for, since these relics are very appreciated in the whole world. According to my research, this tomb has had to be opened twice already in antiquity, both with negative results, and all its treasures must be intact. I have found evidence that they had excavated in the wrong places and possibly could never get past the antechamber. Keep in mind that the air is getting thinner as we enter and possibly, there are many traps to avoid intruders.

- And we are not equally intruders? Worried Wells asked.

- Some people say yes and that these graves should not be desecrated by anyone. My justification for doing so is that at least we are not going to steal anything, since everything we find here will be handed over to the Egyptian government. We are archaeologists, we are not looking for money. The fate of all this is the Cairo museum.

- And you are not afraid of traps and curses?

- Well, now we have the experience accumulated in other open tombs and we know many of the tricks that builders used to prevent intruders from entering the burial chamber. The most important thing for them was to ensure the tranquility of the deceased, of the pharaoh, and for that they used false cameras, even false corpses, which misled thieves for centuries. See, for example, these engravings on the wall depicting seals. For years, researchers have tried to vainly explain what they meant by these animals, extremely far from their normal habitat. But we have come to the conclusion that, in reality, they are keys to open the different doors of the grave. There are three different sets of seals, each in the opposite position, which indicate the movements that we will have to make to the keys to be able to open it.

- And nobody has tried to simply throw the doors down?

- They have tried and they have succeeded, but at the cost of their lives. Every open door abruptly operates thick stones that not only seal the entrance again, but block the exit to the outside to the tomb raiders. Soon you will see numerous skeletons in the corridors that will indicate without a doubt where the thieves died.

- But I thought these skeletons belonged to the guards and workers of the Pharaoh, who ordered they should be buried in his tomb so as not to divulge the secrets to anyone.

- That theory is very imaginative, but lacking credibility. When the tombs were built, everyone knew that there were numerous deadly traps to hunt the intruders but, simultaneously, nobody knew where or how these traps were located. There was never a single architect working on the pyramids, but dozens, and each secretly elaborated their plans that were subsequently destroyed. At that time, it was impossible that anybody could have survived by entering one of these tombs.

-And now?

- Now I hope we have more luck than our predecessors.

CHAPTER 14

AN EMBRYING PERFUME

They moved slowly down a corridor of dusty, rough walls, some with engravings, while the floor was made of large tiles. The corridor was slightly descending and could barely be illuminated by the portable lamps, although the light was enough to warn them that it had reached the end of the corridor, where a solid wall awaited them.

- Well -Wells said- and now what do we do?

- Well now we'll have to throw this wall. Behind it we will find the antechamber -Howard replied.

- How can you be so sure?

- My experience has made me see that all funeral monuments were made under the same principles. We have always met at least three seals before we can reach the burial chamber. The problem, however, is not to pull down the seals one by one until we get to the right place, something relatively easy. The most difficult thing is to find out what kind of traps they have set to prevent us from reaching the tomb of Pharaoh. Each architect made his own traps and there is no key book that tells us how they can be disabled. It is as if we were in an abandoned mine about to collapse on our heads.

- Well -Wells said nervously- If you want, I'll wait for you outside.

- Do not even think about doing it. Everything in these tombs is so well elaborated that they had even foreseen the escape of the possible thieves. Once inside, there is only one option: to reach the end, going back leads inexorably to certain death. Do you see these skeletons? Surely they are people who decided to turn around when they encountered the first difficulty or preferred to leave to seek help. The pharaohs did not want witnesses, nor thieves who returned to try to rob them again. All those who dared to enter had to die, sooner or later, in one way or another.

- You say it as if that death threat did not involve us.

- You must understand that if entering and leaving any pyramid would have been so simple, after so many thousands of years there would not be a single stone left of them. For centuries, the treasures hidden here have tempted people from all countries and if they are still standing it is because most of them have died trying. But do not worry, the experience of our predecessors will be very useful and we have some old documents that make our work easier.

-Look -Carnarvon interrupted- in this corner of the seal must be placed the lever that holds the protective stone. We must move it carefully so that it does not crush us.

-Look Wells -Howard explained- this is one of its deadly traps. Apparently, the wall seems easy to shoot, but if you try to hit it in any area, a thick stone will fall from the ceiling that will crush us. Normally there are three stones, in case there are more thieves who want to try again. If you look at the ground you will notice that at least one of them has already fallen and has been embedded in the sand. With the passing of the centuries there is scarcely any vestige left of the stone and the unhappy one who died crushed by it. But now it would be better to retire.

A solid blow in the specific place indicated by Carnarvon, was enough to activate the first of the traps. A part of the roof moved a few millimeters, but it remained solidly still.

- See, if the blow had been made elsewhere the stone would have fallen on top of us. Now he's still there, waiting for the next person who may try to enter through the wall. In any case, it is very possible that, we also have problems to leave with the one that still remains. We should try to activate the trap from here.

But the attempts to find some signal that indicated without possibility of error where the key was located, were in vain. Most likely, according to his knowledge, that sign was behind the wall, waiting for the thief to try to get out there once in possession of the treasures. Therefore, they had no option but to throw the wall at the risk of having the entire roof falling over them. Armed with a pickaxe of more than three meters they began to pierce the seal little by little, trying to find the small holes that had been left between each stone. This slow, but meticulous work had its reward and soon a dark room was seen behind the hole. Little by little they were opening the wall even more and then they were able to get inside, a place where an intense perfume was perceived. Once the three were inside and after the dim light of the lamps illuminated the room, they found an oriental wall in which a seal was perceived, an unequivocal signal that communicated with another room, possibly the Funeral Chamber. There were also remains of the lifting of a seal on the front wall, which must have communicated with another room, although for unknown reasons that option was discarded. However, on the left end of this front wall were two rough cuts, surrounded by black lines that seemed to represent a door without a seal.

-Come here -said Howard- that little door will surely lead us to an uninteresting place, although it may contain some treasures, all of little importance. The purpose of these false rooms was to mislead the thieves by making them believe that in this tomb there were no more valuable treasures. Thus they forced them to take those crumbs and not find the real ones, those that would help the pharaoh to start a new life in the other world without economic problems.

-What I cannot identify -commented Wells uneasily- is this penetrating aroma in this room, and even less its usefulness. Not pretending to scare you, I would say that it reminds me somewhat of the opium dens that exist in Chinatown in New York.

-Oh, do not worry! -explained Carnarvon very enthusiastic- a small dose of hallucinogens will not make you any bad in these circumstances. Personally I must admit that this scent is making me feel really good and I have even thought I saw in the dark a beautiful Egyptian queen insinuating herself to me.

-I have read something -Wells commented nervously- about the mystique of smells, and it is quite possible that the terrible Pharaonic curses, by which the tomb raiders of the tombs went mad and committed suicide or turned into ruthless assassins, have their origin in the intelligent use of certain essences. We know the ability of Egyptian doctors to mummify their deads, and it is quite possible that with their incredible imagination they found very effective substances to prevent anyone from entering a grave and leaving alive.

-Come on! -Replied Howard, smiling- do not let your imagination fly to confuse an aroma of incense with a deadly perfume. Scientists have never given credit to these legends and have always considered them as alterations produced by hysteria or by the desire to find in those funeral mausoleums things that escape routine.

- What is true, said Carnarvon, is that this devilish perfume has something strange. I begin to feel dizzy and I think it would be convenient for us to go out a bit.

That was the last word he said before collapsing on the ground. In the same way, and with the same rapidity, Wells and Howard fell, without any one even having time to try to leave the antechamber. Immersed in a deep and restless sleep, the three researchers of Egyptian ruins were now unconscious, slowly absorbing the lethal gases from this strange perfume.

The first one that woke up was Wells, after being asleep for an indeterminate period of time, perhaps because it was the first time he inhaled that Egyptian aroma and was not too intoxicated. What he found around him was not the funerary antechamber, which was practically empty, but he was inside a deep well dimly lit coming from the entrance of the well. Above, at least twenty meters high, seemed to be the exit, but the wall was so smooth that any attempt to climb would be unviable. On the other hand, he was alone, his two research colleagues had disappeared and an intense cold was leaving him seriously in pain and without strength. He tried to ask for help, but his throat was completely dry and he could not exhale even a faint moan. Perhaps the same drug that had made him sleep had paralyzed his vocal cords, which would demonstrate the great wisdom that Egyptian architects had then to destroy the profaners of their graves.

The hours passed relentlessly for Wells, who was beginning to consider that his life was coming to an end, since there was no possibility of asking for help or leaving from there by his own means. His only hope was that the time machine would return him abruptly to his time, but according to his calculations that would not happen for two more days and in this two days anything could happen in this strange cave. What would happen if he unfortunately died at that time in the past? Would he also die in 1938? What would happen to his body? Struggling to find some valid explanations for his future. Now, more out of fear than out of scientific interest, Wells tried, again, to climb the walls even though his limited strength did not allow him to climb more than a couple of meters.

Simultaneously with Wells' dramatic problem, Howard had been transported, perhaps by the same people who had locked the writer in that dark well, to a room so small that it did not even allow him to stand. With a height of no more than five feet and without any door that would give him the chance to get out of there, Howard found himself in need of crawling around looking for a possible way out. His most logical reasoning made him believe that if he had been imprisoned there recently there should be some hidden door through which he had been introduced, but he could not find that door anywhere. His imagination, sharpened by the hallucinogen he had inhaled, soon led him to a conclusion that terrified him fully: he had surely been buried in life, walled up, as Edgar Allan Poe had described in one of his novels.

And little by little, what at first was a source of stupor and bewilderment, became a cause of despair, as to the discomfort to be there, just sitting, was added to the rarefied air, now already saturated in carbon dioxide and that produced a terrifying suffocation. He began to dig into the walls with his hands, since his lack of serenity told him that where there had been an entrance before there could be an exit and that everything was a matter of finding it. Soon his nails disappeared and the yolk of bloody fingers kept searching frantically for the possible exit, first frontally and later on the ceiling. The earth was not too hard and allowed him to advance in his attempt, but except for drilling a small hole in the wall he did not get anything else. Soon the pain in his fingers was so deep that he was forced to abandon this task and stay lying on the ground. Dirty and full of blood, plunged into despair, he abandoned himself to his fate.

Carnarvon, on the other hand, had not had better luck than his companions and when he awoke he was inside a dark cave, in which the heat was the most predominant note. Without a single light that allowed him to see his surroundings, he had to slowly feel the rock walls to realize that this place must belong to the interior of some mountain. In less than fifteen minutes, he had managed to delimit the structure and size of the cave, but apart from rocks and suffocating air he found nothing that would allow him to get out of there. His attempts to find out the height of the place were unsuccessful and each attempt to climb the walls, led only to a loud and painful fall to the hard ground.

After an hour of futile attempts to find a way out of there, Carnarvon tried to calm down to reason about the causes that had led him there.

At the same time, he wondered where his companions might be, and tried to find a reason why someone had drugged him and locked him in such a deadly grave. His ramblings made him see that it would have been easier to kill them all, since for the defenders of these tombs they were nothing more than desecrators of the eternal rest of the pharaohs. Perhaps - and this new frightening conclusion gave him goose bumps - they wanted to give him a macabre lesson for daring to disturb the sleep of such illustrious dead, almost gods, and sought that his death was a prolonged and painful agony. Soon and as happened elsewhere with his companions, sitting on the floor he reviewed the circumstances that could have led him there, while waiting resigned his deadly fate.

The hours passed and the three were immersed in a long dream that lasted a long time, in which the presence of the beyond, with ghosts and spirits included enveloped them, and all were transported to a dark place where suicide was the better alternative to avoid the pain that was already beginning to be unbearable. Screaming, crying and sometimes banging their heads against the wall, they tried to take their own lives in order to escape the misfortune that had so brutally come to them.

And it was Wells who first came out of that awful place. Sweating intensely and with terror still reflected on his face, he opened his eyes and found himself back in the antechamber of the pyramid, safe and sound. Soon he realized that everything had been a horrible nightmare, probably generated by that strange perfume. There, on the floor, his two companions were still asleep, their bodies equally drenched in sweat and moaning intensely, an unequivocal sign that they were still mired in the terror of sleep. He hurriedly shook them intensely so that they woke up, which he achieved almost effortlessly, although he had to ask them to calm down again and again to make them understand that everything had been just a dream.

- Do you still think that perfume was here, permeating the air, by chance? Wells asked to Howard.

- I do not know, although it is possible that everything was due to this rarefied air.

- That rarefied air has already disappeared, just as the aromas of a perfume disappear. The most logical thing is to think that these aromas have been released just when we have opened the seal and that they were there waiting to be inhaled by the first defiler of the grave, to unbalance his mind and make him live terrible nightmares.

- Well, but that scent was not lethal and I do not see its use if it all comes down to a bad nightmare. We are still here, safe and sound, eager to continue our explorations.

- You must take into account the time in which these pyramids were made. The people of that time were more superstitious than us and with their gods they also had a large number of demons. They believed faithfully in the afterlife and in the spirits. A nightmare like the one we have lived now should be enough to make them flee quickly from here and not try again their desire to steal.

-Fortunately -said Carnarvon -they did not have the presence of rational explorers like us. In my case, I have no desire to abandon the treasure hunt. I think the time has come to return to our work, unless some of you decide to end your exploration.

- (Wells, now more excited) I would not miss the end of this story for the world.

Although in that place they found offerings of food, some weapons, two statues and some clothes, none of them wanted to touch those objects, since their main interest was in the tomb of the pharaoh and in the treasure that would allow him to reach splendidly to the other lifetime. Their explorations led them to locate the door that should lead them to the burial chamber, the place where the tomb of Tutankhamun was most certainly located. All the most reliable signs were right on the front wall, where a slight variation in the color of the wall indicated that the materials used there were different from the rest. Provided with their little pegs and trying to look exclusively for a thin line indicating the presence of a door, they began to scratch the entire wall gently.

Again it was Wells who pulled his companions out of his reverie when he told them joyfully that there, right on the left side, almost touching the corner, was the unmistakable mark of a door. From that moment and once they had delimited the outline, began a patient but insistent work to enlarge the furrow that should release the door. None of them expected to find a hinge or something that would allow them to easily move that heavy door made of huge stones, but at least they already knew that there should be a mechanism that would act as a lock. Soon that system was discovered in the superior part, consisting of a small and simple block that once pushed would release four more that would allow, finally, to enter without problems in the annexed chamber.

- I hope - Carter said something uneasy - that there are no new hallucinogenic perfumes here.

-I am very afraid -Carnarvon replied- that this room contains neither perfumes nor treasures. See this furniture so bare and useless; no pharaoh would sit on such furniture. There are hardly any offerings of food, nor any treasure of value.

- What explanation is there for this? It is not reasonable that a camera has been built without any use for the pharaoh. Maybe it's just an antechamber that leads to another.

-Or a new deadly trap for the profaners- said nervous Carter. If so, I would recommend extreme caution when touching any object and make a discreet withdrawal to return to the antechamber. At least that one we already know is safe.

His words had barely ended when an intense crunch made him mute. The whole chamber began to move, while sand began to fall through holes in the ceiling. In a few seconds there were already six holes that vomited the unsettling sand and it seemed to presage that this room would soon fill up and bury the three researchers alive.

Initially stunned, but somewhat more serene by their experience with these deadly problems, they tried eagerly to plug the holes that pushed the sand into the chamber.

-It's useless! -Cried Carnarvon- this sand comes directly from the desert and is bearing a pressure of thousands of tons. There is no human force that can stop it. We must leave as soon as possible.

But the designers of that pyramid had foreseen all the possible escapes and when they returned to the exit door, in their place there was only a thick stone recently fallen from the roof. His only hope of escape was blocked, while the ground was inexorably filled with hot sand. At that moment none of them stood still and frantically searched for any sign or place that would indicate a new exit door, while their feet were already covered by sand. The speed with which the camera was filled was very high, but not so high that they did not have time to think about his immediate death.

Everything seemed to have been carefully planned by the builders so that the profaners would have enough time to endure a slow agony, adequate punishment for their audacity to interrupt the Pharaoh's dream. The thieves - in this case our three researchers - should mentally unbalance while they saw the sand rise up their bodies, ending their days with a slow and terrible death, fully aware of what it means to be buried in life.

The minutes passed relentlessly and terrifyingly, more quickly than they would now wish, and soon from their lips no more moans came out, being replaced by prayers and prayers. To the memories towards their relatives and the philosophical phrases to prepare with more serenity before their tragic destiny, followed words of consolation of one another, once they had abandoned all hope of leaving alive. But in this tomb of solitude, everything that was said barely served to remove that mortal anguish, exacerbated because the pressure of the sand around their bodies began to hinder their breathing.

Carnarvon soon collapsed emotionally and began to scream, first asking for help and then cursing his job and the circumstances that had brought him to that place. He strongly blamed Carter for not foreseeing these traps and accused him with great insults of incompetent egotist, leaving some loose words to laugh at Wells and his stupid tale about the time machine. He asked Wells, in a desperate attempt to get rid of his fear, to activate his machine to get him out of there and crying with despair he was silent when the sand completely covered his face, silenced for good.

Later, fate was equally implacable with Wells, who fortunately managed to find some reason for consolation in this mortal moment to think that possibly his time machine would rescue him just at the last moment. It had already happened on other occasions and he was sure that these circumstances would happen again, and that again he would go back to his old basement to plan the next trips in time.

His thoughts were interrupted when the sand entered sharply through his nose and an intense choke plunged him into despair. Short of air and totally suffocated, he tried desperately to surface, while looking imploringly at Carter. When it was completely hidden by the sand the silence was made in that place, since Carter had fainted long ago by the pressure of the sand in his chest. He was the luckiest of the three to not be aware of the horror of being buried alive.

CHAPTER 15

THE WORLD OF THE DEAD

It is not easy to know what happens in the other life, since we still have no record of anyone who has returned from the beyond to tell us their experiences. Although some people have had heart attacks for a few minutes and have told mystical experiences about what happens on that threshold between life and death, their experiences refer precisely to an antechamber, not to the real other life, if it exists.

That's why we should not be surprised that when Wells, Carnarvon and Carter arrived at that place where time and space do not exist, they spent a few seconds analyzing where they were. In their faces there was no fear, only doubts, while their bodies seemed not to exist in the absence of any pain or negative sensation. Although they looked at each other and tried to know where they were, they were not able to articulate a word, not even to express joy. If they were dead the sensation was not unpleasant, and if they were still alive they did not want to know what had happened to them. They got up slowly and still stunned, looked now in more detail around.

-It is incredible! -Said Carter excitedly-, we are back in the annexed chamber, but there is no sign of sand and the door that we open is still open. What happened?

-I am afraid- said Carnarvon- that we have returned to being victims of hallucinations caused by the perfumes that fill these places.

-The strange thing about this- Carter went on- is that it seems that we all have the same nightmares, which is something even more incredible.

-People- Wells tried to explain, "have been able to build such wonders, they should perfectly dominate the world of drugs. We should not be surprised that his knowledge of hallucinogens was infinitely superior to ours.

- I'm glad to be alive, but if all their traps are reduced to making us have a bad nightmare from time to time, I do not see much wisdom in it. If what they were trying to do was prevent us from reaching the tomb of Pharaoh, it would be enough to have put physical deadly traps, like arrows or crushing rocks- said Carter.

-We have not reached the sarcophagus yet- replied Wells uneasily. I think the best traps are still waiting for us and I am afraid that some of them may be more forceful. Since in this place we have not found anything of real value, I think it is time keep search for the true entrance to the burial chamber.

He did not need to insist much on his request, as everyone had the same desire to get out of there. A quick glance at the antechamber indicated that only on the eastern wall could the seal that covered the entrance to the burial chamber be found. This time the speed with which the wall was bitten was much higher than expected, because they were more concerned about the presence of new hallucinogens than the possible collapse of the roof. Fortunately, this new seal was not as resistant to pickaxes as the previous ones, which indicated that at this point and if the tomb raiders had managed to arrive safe and sound, the architects knew that nothing would stop them now, at least nothing solid.

When the voluminous seal that completely covered the eastern wall finally fell, the three tomb raiders remained for a few minutes without daring to enter, not so much because of the absence of light inside, but because of the fear of breathing again the terrifying gases. No one was convinced that he could survive a new dream, especially because his tired hearts had been beating too fast for hours. Suffering from a persistent arrhythmia, sweating intensely on the forehead and with an emotional state close to a shock, they all were tempted to leave right now, a more pleasant solution than to enter this new chamber. Fortunately, and although they all thought the same, their thoughts remained in their mind and slowly entered the pharaoh's burial chamber.

This new room was lower with respect to the previous one and this made Carter think that, at some point of construction, there was no thought of locating the burial chamber in this place and originally was built in line with the north wall of the antechamber. There were marks on these bricks, as well as limestone, plaster, and paintings, but they did not find any reasonable explanation for this impractical change.

Once the lamps properly illuminated the room, they found on the north wall a painting that was supposed to represent King Tutankhamun. The painting showed him assuming the entrance into his new life, dressed as he was usually dressed and embraced by the god Osiris. On the eastern wall was shown his funeral, with his head covered with garlands and the coffin pulled by a sleigh, in addition to some hieroglyphic texts that explained who were the most senior officers in the palace. Finally, on the south wall, they showed him receiving the welcome to the new life from the hand of the god Anubis and the goddess Hathor, as well as other minor gods.

All the decoration was magnificent, appropriated for an earthly god. Adorned with an abundance of golden motifs, the multi-colored paintings had stood the test of time. And there, almost in the middle of the room, was a huge quartzite sarcophagus. Although the finding filled the aspirations and dreams of the explorers, none dared to touch him, and even less to approach him. The possibility of new hallucinogenic gases in the environment was present in their minds and with it the terror.

The first one that approached was Carter, more accustomed than his companions to enter and rummage in dark places of the past. Once he slowly removed the dust and mildew accumulated on top, he began, now with the help of his companions, to try and find a way to open the lid of the sarcophagus. The work was slow, laborious and delicate, but soon they got the reward and the lid was deposited on the floor. Suddenly, Carnarvon shouted:

- Damn! Something has bitten me in the neck!

- Look, there was a mosquito inside the sarcophagus! - Wells said nervously, pointing to the insect that was already running away.

- But how is it possible that it could have survived so many years locked up, without air or food?

-Do not be surprised, Carnarvon- said Carter. That mosquito had enough air here to live hundreds of years longer, given its small size and, in addition, it is possible that there is somewhere some parasitic air intake to keep oxygen in the proper proportion. And about food you should keep in mind that a corpse has enough meat to provide it with food without problems.

-Corpse? What corpse? There is nothing here, just a granite stone.

-Be patient. What you see is surely hiding a coffin and possibly the pharaoh is buried here. Help me move the stone.

- I still don't understand how a mosquito has been able to live almost 5,000 years, taking into account that those we know barely live for a few days.

-Good question. I would like to know the answer.

Once they left the heavy slab on the ground, the only thing they found inside the coffin was a new coffin and inside this one another.

Discouraged, they abandoned their work and preferred to eat something before continuing with their research. Once the forces recovered, Carter investigated again what seemed to be simply an unimportant box, although once scratched the paint that covered it was found with a sheath of pure gold.

-I found it! He shouted exultantly. Here is the true tomb of Tutankhamun.

And he was right, since once the golden lid was patiently lifted and the black resin that covered the coffin was removed internally, the young pharaoh's mummy appeared, his face and shoulders covered by a gold mask, precious stones and blue glass. Crowned by a vulture head that symbolized sovereignty over Upper Egypt and the eyes of quartz and obsidian, the face that represented Tutankhamun had a splendid beauty. When they partially discovered the mummy they found an embalming oil that was a mixture of essences of anise, thyme, oregano and propolis, together with tar and exudates from the body of the deceased, perhaps blood and lymph. Along with these compounds were others, alkaloids among them, whose mission in embalming was not clear and could be the substances that had reacted over the centuries and that caused the delusions of the explorers.

- What a magnificent work of conservation! Carnarvon commented, although very impractical.

- Egyptians and their cult of the dead must not be judged hastily. The main reason for the embalming was to ensure a pleasant life in the other world and that is why they considered it appropriate to use so much care in it. Many of these resins contained hallucinogenic substances and thus could provide their dead with a very special state of mind at the time of reincarnation.

- And to us the entrance by the fast route in the other life - ironic commented Wells.

-Guys!- Carter interrupted- I do not want to be an alarmist, but I smell a certain perfume that worries me. Very possibly we are approaching another phantasmagoric dream of which I have a feeling that we will not escape with as much fortune as in the other two occasions.

- No, not this time! Carnarvon shouted. Let's get handkerchiefs on our nose to mitigate the vapors and let's get into the treasure room. If the hallucinogens have left the sarcophagus it is very possible that they volatilize very quickly.

All with handkerchiefs that they carried in their pockets blocking their nose quickly entered the treasure chamber, a fourth annex that, curiously, was not closed. There they found, though now with little enthusiasm, ritual divans, jewels, amulets, wine jars, pottery, tools and lamps, as well as wicker baskets, alabaster chests, musical instruments and dried edibles.

- How much wonder hidden in a single room! Carter said cheerfully. It would take a lifetime to classify all this and study its correct use. I think we can learn more from the Egyptians by analyzing these objects, than by studying all the Egyptology books written so far.

- Can we take these treasures to our country? Carnarvon asked.

-Not at all. The Egyptian authorities have given me permission to excavate here, but with the clear warning that everything I found would belong to Egypt and that any other issue would be considered an act of sacrilegious robbery. They also warned me about what happened to grave robbers and hidden treasures if they ended up in their prisons. All these objects are planned to be moved to the Cairo museum, first on a train and then on a steamer ship that will take them downstream to their destination.

- But won't they even let you analyze the pharaoh's mummy? Wells asked.

- I think this cannot be done at the moment. The first thing we have to do is classify everything we have found here, draw pictures of the hieroglyphics on the walls and draw an exact shot of the tomb. We have to make sure, and assure them, that everything will be delivered to the Egyptian authorities as we have found it.

A noise from the burial chamber startled them. First they looked at each other in astonishment, then recoiled instinctively, and then awaited events that did not come. Pale, with a face disheveled and sweating intensely, the three investigators did not even want to talk, perhaps not to alert anyone or anything about their presence. Carter approached Wells and quietly whispered in his ear:

- Maybe they are bandits or grave robbers who have followed us and who patiently wait for us to show them the way to the treasure.

- But who knows you are here?

- (Always whispering) Only the director of the Cairo museum and the Chief of Police. Everything has been kept in absolute secrecy. Even the vehicle that brought us here was driven by the Chief of Police.

-Not to mention, -Carnarvon went on to explain- that there is a strict surveillance a hundred kilometers from here so that no one can approach.

When the noise inside the funeral chamber became louder, no one dared to keep talking. Carnarvon, something braver and more determined than the others, was the first one who dared to investigate, being followed somewhat further by Wells and Carter. What they saw there was not usual and was against any scientific conjecture: Tutankhamun's mummy, still covered in black resin and mold, was sitting in his own grave, with his eyes directed exactly at the three investigators.

-Hell! Exclaimed Carter- someone tells me that what I'm seeing is not true.

- (Carnarvon, more serene) Well, well, do not panic, it's really a natural phenomenon. All corpses suffer a large dilation of their tissues when subjected to a sudden change in temperature and they usually move and appear to sit.

- But this mummy has been dead for thousands of years! Retorted Carter, still frightened.

- Look, ignorant friend, the Egyptian mummies belong to the desert, a place where it hardly rains. When we opened the tomb there has been a sudden climate change here and this has caused this reaction that seems to scare you so much.

-Well, now I would like you to explain to me, -Wells shouted almost- the reason why the mummy is rising as if it was alive.

Certainly, and to everyone's astonishment, the mummy of King Tutankhamun, majestic and proud, had already risen from the sarcophagus and stood staring at everyone. At this time, no one was able to articulate a word or make a decision. When a few seconds passed, it was again Carter who took the reins of the group to explain that...

- Look, all this is not possible that is real. What you see now is not a freshly dead person, with the whole body still intact. Mummies have no brains, no intestines and no eyes. Everything is extracted and filled later with myrrh, cassia and perfumes of all kinds. There is no way that they can keep standing.

-Well, the only explanation is that it's another hallucination -Wells suggested, now calmer.

-True. Possibly we are immersed in another dreadful dream provoked by those devilish perfumes. I suggest we pinch ourselves hard to get out as soon as possible -Carter replied.

But while the three investigators proceeded to pinch their bodies and slapping each other in the face in an attempt to get out of what they supposed was a nightmare, the mummy began to walk slowly towards them, while showing bloodshot eyes that did not foresee anything good. This forced them to slowly retreat to the only possible exit, the treasure chamber itself, located just behind them. But with each step that was taken backwards the mummy made another one towards them, so that in less than two minutes they were all already inside the treasure chamber.

Cornered among the fabulous objects, our friends did not find any way to reach the door to make a quick escape to the outside, and any attempt to deceive the mummy was useless. Attempts to wake up from that hypothetical macabre dream also failed and all they got was a lot of bruises and small wounds. On this occasion, the dream had become reality.

There was an especially tense moment when the mummy stood motionless looking at the three tomb raiders, at the same time that they also stared intently into his eyes. No one moved a millimeter, nor was there any noise that disturbed that terrifying moment. Suddenly, the mummy turned discreetly towards the wall of the entrance and gave a strong slap to the wall that echoed disturbingly. The whole room seemed to begin to crack in its foundations, until a thick marble stone fell from the ceiling and completely sealed the entrance door. Then, they were all locked in the treasure room.

-It's not possible! Tell me that it is not possible and that it is all a bad dream! Whimpered Carter almost crying.

- (Wells, anguished) He has buried us in life! That door must weigh several tons.

- (Carter, very nervous) We must do something right away, before the air is gone.

- But that monster remains imperturbable in front of us..

His words had barely ended when the mummy began a slowly fading and as if it were the invisible man described by Wells in one of his novels, he disappeared little by little from the place. From that moment, where before there was a mummy coming from the Egypt of the pharaohs, now there was nothing.

-It has disappeared! Wells shouted.

- (Carter) I think now I understand what just happened to us. We have suffered a new hallucination, the darkest of all. That mummy has never existed, except in his grave. Our imagination has made us believe that it had risen, forced us to retreat to this point and one of us, no matter who, has activated the trap that has caused the descent of that door.

-Do you mean -Carnarvon asked- that we have buried ourselves in life? Was it all a new hallucination caused by those damn perfumes? It is not possible that we are so stupid.

-There's nothing stupid -Carter added- when you're under the influence of a hallucinogen. We have behaved like people suffering from delirium tremens or who believe that they attend the vision of the devil or the spirits. For us everything was absolutely real, so real that it has forced us to do things as macabre as this.

-And what can we do now? Wells sighed.

- That slab is impossible to move, especially because the desert sand has sealed it permanently. If this camera does not have another new exit, I believe that our destiny is already written and that the word "end" has arrived.

- Well, let's find another way out before the fire of the lamps is over and we are left in the dark -said Carnarvon, as he began to explore the walls.

- Sorry to disappoint you, dear friend, but the Egyptian tombs have no exit door, only one to entry. There is no emergency back door and when you want to leave you have to do it by the same place you entered, something that is now impossible.

- What do you suggest?

- Let's prepare ourselves to die. After the two previous experiences, I believe that we are now better able to accept our mortal destiny - Carter said with absolute serenity.

These words were followed by a few glances between them, also many tears and some acts of desperation to find a way out that certainly did not exist. On this occasion the nightmare was a reality and one could only expect death, ironically just the same day they had found the great treasure. The hours were passing inexorably and the three lived the phases through which all humans pass before they die: struggle to survive, irritability for fate, and submissive acceptance of death. And so, when the last lamp consumed its oil, the entire chamber was immersed in total darkness, while the silence became even more terrifying.

CHAPTER 16

THE END

Wells never knew how much time he spent in that tenebrous room, or whether he was actually asleep or awake awaiting his death. When he opened his eyes he was in the time machine, firmly anchored in his old basement. Never before had he been so happy to return to his time, but soon his thoughts traveled again to his two companions in misfortune: Carnarvon and Carter, two researchers to whom technology had not saved them from death.

Immersed in sadness, tired and hurt by the hazardous trip to Egypt, he dropped abruptly into the best sofa in his library, while trying to put his ideas in order. At that time, he realized the great loneliness that was pursuing him, unable to find a companion who followed him excited in his travels in time. Nobody gave credit to his projects and not even those who had already traveled with him considered that these trips had been a reality.

A dream or an illusion, that's the only thing that these trips have been for them. They are ignorant people who can only see what their body can see or touch, as if dreams and imagination were not always present with us, he told himself.

At that moment a spark, a light, crossed his mind and he ran to look in the history books a historical fact that he needed to clarify as soon as possible. He searched the history of the Egyptian pyramids, especially in the pages that spoke of the discovery of the tomb of King Tutankhamun. There, obviously, appeared Lord Carnarvon and Howard Carter, both showing the World the treasures they had discovered in the Egyptian tomb. They also talked about the tremendous hallucinations that occurred to them and how they had been about to die because of them. H. G. Wells was not even mentioned, perhaps because they also thought that it had been a product of their delusions, which is not surprising considering that he disappeared suddenly from there.

The information also mentioned the curse of the pharaohs and the death of Carnarvon on April 6, 1923, as well as the suicide of Lord

Westbury and his son, both participants of new investigations in that tomb. Other mysterious deaths related to Tutankhamun were those of Arthur Weigall, Archibald Douglas and Mace, as well as that of Carnarvon's half-brother and his own wife, Elisabeth Carnarvon. The only one that remained alive for many years was Howard Carter.

The conclusion that Wells drew from all this is that this last burial in life had been another nightmare and when his friends woke up they found two surprises: they were alive and Wells had disappeared.

During the years that followed, H. G. Wells never made another trip and tried unsuccessfully to perfect his time machine, in a desperate attempt to master it and to travel without problems to the past and, perhaps, to the future. But with each new project came a new disappointment and after numerous failures and seeing how life and strength escaped him little by little, he decided to totally destroy his time machine, as stealthily as he had built it. Since no one had ever believed in his invention, no one should benefit when he had died. Humanity, with its habitual deaf ears to great innovations, had lost its great opportunity to positively influence events.

WHAT HAPPENED AFTERWARDS?

H. G. Wells
Herbert George Wells

In his last works, "Autobiographical experiment" in 1935 and "The mind in the limit of his resources" in 1945, he no longer spoke about a hopeful future as a sample of the pessimism that invaded him.

His discouraging predictions began to set in 1933 and if we review his stories we can always see an apocalyptic tone, a Humanity that likes to destroy what has just been built. He tried to inculcate the idea of a new kind of world consciousness, governed by a single government, which should take care of all wars to achieve a peaceful world state. This government should provide a welfare state superior to anything known. He was convinced that through scientific progress the whole world would be able to live in peace and free from old hatreds.

Demoralized by the impossibility of being able to demonstrate that his time machine was a reality, he abandoned science-fiction literature in his later years to write about political events and social problems. These works, logically, hardly had repercussion among the public, especially because they were already catastrophists and very far from the optimistic tone of the previous ones. Now, Humanity was no longer moving towards a better world, with the united countries, but only saw terrible wars, hunger and much pain.

Herbert George Wells died in 1946, eight years after his travels in time and although he could never prove that they were a reality, his literary work was admired during the years that followed his death. Of the majority of their novels several cinematographic versions were made, reaching great relief "The war of the worlds", "The island of doctor Moreau", "The invisible man" and "The time machine", all considered already like classics indisputable of fantasy cinema.

His great illusion was the trips in time, and for the majority of the fans in this work is summarized all the fantasy of Wells, as well as much of the social criticism that worried him. Unfortunately, it showed us a terrible world that would come sooner or later and predicted that 30 million years would come the death of our planet. Then we will see.

Mata-hari
Margaretha Geertruida Zelle

Born in Leewarden, the Netherlands, on August 7, 1876, she married Rudolph Macleod, a Dutch army captain, stationed in East Java. They had two children, but one of them was poisoned by one of his servants, in revenge as Rudolph had raped one of his daughters. The couple returned to Holland, where they divorced soon after, leaving for Paris. With her knowledge of Indian customs, plus some oriental gems in her body, Margaretha invented a new family, this time belonging to a sacred Indian temple, followers, therefore, of the Brahaman doctrine. An adequate artistic training in the rituals of the Kandaswami, the sacred Hindu dance, surrounded her with a mystical aureole, especially attractive because she danced it naked.

At her death, shot in Paris, the famous earring (they said it was a present from a woman who loved her), was jealously hidden and she was last seen at the Dorot auction in Paris, in 1952, being bought by a woman who claimed that she had also been a spy.

Orson Welles
George Orson Welles

After his contact with H. G. Wells, he continued to make films with unequal commercial success. The film "Citizen Kane" was filmed almost in secret because of the attempts of the millionaire Randolph Hearst to prevent it, and its release was almost a resounding commercial failure, as well as "The Magnificent Ambersons".

Passionate about Spain, where he filmed "Chimes at midnight", he tried to make a living writing and sometimes as a bullfighter, but fortunately he continued with the cinema to bequeath us works like "Othello", "Moby Dick" (here as an actor), "The long, hot summer" (also as an actor),"Touch of Evil"(actor and director) or" Chimes at midnight ", among others.

Married to Rita Hayworth, whom he directed in "The Lady from Shanghai", he was considered in life as a conflictive director and for that reason we could affirm that he was left out of the big projects. His last work as a director was with "F for Fake", although later he continued to intervene in film as an actor until 1985, in the movie "Someone to Love". At his death, on October 10, 1985, his work gained an amazing prestige and today he is considered one of the greatest geniuses of cinema. He is buried in a private ranch near

Seville, a place he loved especially because he had been very happy there when he was young.

Humphrey Bogart

Humphrey DeForest Bogart

Bogart made his last film in 1956, a drama about the world of boxing entitled "The harder they fall ".

After a brief rest period, in February 1956 he underwent a surgical operation to remove a malignant cancer of the esophagus. Apparently, he recovered and gained some weight. Unfortunately, a few months later, in November of the same year, he had to enter Samaritan Good Hospital to treat a new growth of the cancerous tumor that was causing pressure on an extremely painful nerve. After surgery, he was sent home, but he never recovered. Bogart died at two ten on January 14, 1957, in the bedroom of his home in Beverly Hills, Hollywood.

The burial of Humphrey Bogart was logically moving and well organized. The first car was a limousine occupied by Lauren Bacall and on each side one of her children. John Huston was also there. All the way to the church the crowds filled the streets and followed the coffin with their eyes. There were already hundreds of cars parked around the church and although there was no one crying, everyone had a handkerchief in their hand, aware that tears would soon come. Everyone was quiet, respectful, and some had flowers.

The funerals were held behind closed doors, although loudspeakers were placed outside so that people could follow the prayers. Lauren took her children by the hand, pulled them out of the limousine and entered the church. Huston stayed outside, along with eight hundred other friends who had come to say goodbye. There were Gary Cooper, Charles Boyer, Tony Martin, Gregory Peck, Marlene Dietrich, Ida Lupino, Howard Duff, Danny Kaye, and of course, Kate Hepburn and Spencer Tracy. Sinatra also wanted to attend the funeral, but he had a very severe contract with his nightclub that prevented him from being absent.

A priest named Kermit said some moving words about Humphrey. Later John Huston arrived and added a short speech: "Bogart is really irreplaceable. There will never be someone like him". Spencer Tracy was also scheduled to speak, but gave up at the last minute because he was not sure he could talk without crying.

But what almost nobody knew was that Bogart's body was not there, as it had been incinerated. Years ago he had expressed his will with the following reasoning during the funeral of his friend Mark Hellinger:

"Once one is gone, it's gone for good. I hate funerals. They are not made for the one who is dead, but for those who stay and can still enjoy living. When I die, I do not want any burial. I prefer cremation that is very clean, and in the end I want my ashes to spread across the Pacific. My friends can build a monument or tell stories if that is their wish, but I do not want any mourning. When I die, I'll be just a wake. "

Unfortunately, when everything was ready for cremation the authorities said it was illegal to spread the ashes on the sea, which caused a serious upset to Lauren Bacall who wanted Bogie to return to the sea he loved so much. Finally he was cremated and his ashes were placed in an urn in the Memorial Garden, in the Forest Cemetery. Along with the ashes was the golden whistle that the spouses had used in their first film together. The initials "B & B" were inscribed on the whistle. At twelve thirty that day, in the studios of the Warner Bros., a minute of silence was observed for Humphrey Bogart.

Groucho Marx

Julius Henry Marx

Over time, this grump was the most famous of the Brothers, mainly due to the popularity that quickly reached with his works in comedy. Groucho interpreted movies, narrated stories, wrote books, presented television programs, danced and even sang for many years, creating a school that even today nobody has been able to take away the leadership. He won several awards for his work including an Oscar, an Emmy, and the title of Master of Arts and Letters of France.

Groucho was a devoted author (having written six books already gave him that category -according to him-, the first of them entitled "Camas") and a renowned screenwriter. In 1937 his work (written together with Krasna Normand) "The King and the Showgirl", had a great success.

As they say, Groucho was happier when he was working on one of these literary projects and that is why his books deserve a much deeper revision than his films. Of special interest are "The letters of Groucho", "Memoirs of a mangy lover" and "Groucho and me".

The end of Groucho's professional life was marked by the decreasing surplus value of the Marx Brothers, although over the years there has been a revival of interest in his films. It seemed that new generation was interested in the works of these three brothers who made their ancestors laugh.

His personal life in the later years was marked by the conflict between his son Arthur and his accountant Erin Fleming, who fought hard for control over Groucho's income and finally for his will and the worldwide rights to his works. This period has been analyzed carefully by Charlotte Chandler in the book "Hello, I'm leaving" and reviewed by Steve Stoliar in another similar work. In 1974 he was awarded an honorary Oscar.

From 1971 until his death in 1977, he was sentimentally attached to his secretary Erin Fleming. He died in Hollywood on August 20, 1977.

Al Capone

Alphonse Gabriel Capone

When Johnny Torrio was seriously wounded Capone took command of his band, making the February 24, 1929, the Valentine's Day Massacre, although he had the wise decision to leave that day to Florida and entrust that mission to his henchmen. A month later appeared before the Grand Jury and although he was not found any evidence that could blame him for his crimes, was arrested for contempt of the Supreme Court and sentenced to one year in prison. But his lawyers prevented the execution of the sentence, and paying a fine of $ 5,000 was immediately released.

Two months later he was judged again, along with his personal guard, and all ended up in jail accused of carrying arms without a license. Although he should have been in jail until the following year, his good behavior, and probably also his money, provided him with several exits, including the one that gave rise to this story.

In 1931 sufficient evidence was gathered to accuse him of tax evasion and he was sentenced to eleven years in prison, plus the payment of almost $ 300,000 in fines. His continuous insults to the court in the numerous trials that took place, only served to increase his sentence and his prison years.

When he finally got free, he was already a decrepit being, sick with syphilis, and was admitted to the Baltimore hospital to treat his dementia. Confined in his Florida home, he completely abandoned his public and criminal life, being considered mentally incapable in 1946 when his doctor and psychiatrist diagnosed that he had a mentality no higher than a 12-year-old child.

Alfonso Capone died of pneumonia at his home in Isla de Palma on January 25, 1947, accompanied by his wife and family.

Lord Carnarvon

George Edward Stanhope Molyneux Herbert

He died on April 6, 1923, a few months after having first entered the tomb of Tutankhamun. According to the coroner, death came as a result of the bite of a mosquito. Then his half-brother Aubrey Herbert killed himself and six years later Carnarvon's wife died, also because of the bite of an insect.